10: JAIMINI AND THE MYSTERY OF EVI BLIGH

"I think you must have got me mixed up with someone else," Evi smiled, "because, you see, I never even went outside this morning. I stayed in at break time."

"Well... We only wanted to help..." Luce began to say, but I reckoned that it was about time we called it a day, because we were getting nowhere fast.

"What's going on, Jaimes?" Luce whispered loudly the moment we were back with the others. "She's lying, she is. What did you drag me away for? I wanted to find out more."

"Because she's acting very mysteriously and obviously doesn't want us involved..."

Also in the Café Club series by Ann Bryant

10: JAIMINI AND THE MYSTERY OF EVI BLIGH

Ann Bryant

Hippo

Scholastic Children's Books,
Commonwealth House, 1–19 New Oxford Street,
London WC1A 1NU, UK
a division of Scholastic Ltd
London ~ New York ~ Toronto ~ Sydney ~ Auckland

First published by Scholastic Ltd, 1997

Copyright © Ann Bryant, 1997

ISBN 0 590 19388 0

Typeset by TW Typesetting, Midsomer Norton, Avon

Printed by Cox & Wyman Ltd, Reading, Berks.

Chapter 1

Hi, I'm Jaimini. I live in a small town called Cableden and I go to Cableden Comprehensive, along with my five really good friends. We're all in year eight and we're all thirteen. We also all work in *The Café* on Cableden High Street. You see, the café is owned by Jan Geeson, who is the aunt of one of these friends of mine.

The way it works is that we all take turns. One person does Monday after school, one Tuesday, etc and one lucky person does Saturday. Saturday's a longer stint and therefore a better earner. That's why we have a rota which changes every week – so that we all get to do a Saturday.

Let me tell you about my friends. I'll start with Luce, because she's my best friend – for my sins! Luce spends her life falling into trouble, then climbing out of it only to go tumbling into another lot. Unfortunately, she often drags me

1

into it with her. Actually, if I'm honest, it's lovely to have a best friend like Luce because she makes life so interesting. Her real name is Lucy Edmunson and we call her the crazy one. She even looks crazy, with her mass of strawberry-blonde curls, her green eyes, her freckles and her weird and wonderful earrings.

Tash, short for Natasha Johnston, is the peace-maker. She has to have everything running smoothly and happily all around her, otherwise she gets in a state. She's kind and understanding and it's impossible to fall out with her. *I* think so, anyway. She's got quite short dark hair, bright eyes and a lovely smile.

Fen is Tash's best friend. Fen is short for Fenella Brooks and she's the ambitious one. It was Fen who got the whole Café Club going in the first place. That wasn't as straightforward as it sounds. Our parents weren't a hundred per cent over the moon about us taking on such a big commitment, and I can't say it's always smooth running even now, but it's brilliant fun and you feel very grown up working in a café. Fen is thin and quite tall with fair to medium hair that goes down to her shoulders. She's also got freckles.

Leah Bryan is the musician. Leah plays the violin and the piano to a very high level. She's exceptionally talented, but *she* doesn't think she is. No matter how much we all tell her, she just shrugs and says anyone could do what she does if they spent the same amount of time at it. That's rubbish, of course! Leah has got a very calm face, very clear skin, and very pale, long straight hair. Luce is totally jealous of all this and would die to look like Leah, even though I keep trying to tell her that if she was dead, Leah's looks wouldn't be an awful lot of use to her.

Andy Sorrell is Leah's best friend. Andy's real name is Agnès, which you pronounce *Ann–yes*, but we've always called her Andy for short. She's half French and half English. Her dad is the English half, although funnily enough he works in France and so he's away a lot. I think Andy's secretly quite relieved that he's away so much because he's the most scary person I've come across. We call Andy the daring one and yet the one thing that scares her is her own dad! Nothing else fazes her at all. She might be small and slight in build, with very short dark hair and huge dark eyes, but she's got enormous courage.

I suppose, out of us all, my colouring is the most like Andy's, though I'm darker than her because my dad's black and my mum's white. My mum's actually quite blonde and people always think I'm adopted when they see us together, but if my dad's there too, they soon get the picture. My hair is as long and straight as Leah's but it's black. Luce fluctuates between wanting my looks

3

and wanting Leah's looks. She really is crazy, that girl!

I've been putting off telling you what the others all call me. That's because I get really embarrassed about it, but anyway, I've got to tell you sometime, so here goes. I'll introduce myself properly.

I am Jaimini Riva (pronounced *Jay-m-nee Reever*) and I'm supposed to be the brainy one!

There, I told you it was embarrassing, so I'll move quickly on to something which happened today that made me *very* puzzled.

It was the beginning of morning break and I reached into my school bag for this magazine called *Our Times*. I'd bought it specially because in it there was a competition to write a story about any environmental subject. One of the English teachers at school first noticed the competition, and it didn't take long for the whole English department to get involved and start encouraging us all to enter. I really wanted to enter the competition because the prize was five hundred pounds as well as the chance to see your work published. Also, you only had to wait a few weeks for the results to come out.

The trouble was, when I searched through my bag the magazine wasn't there, and I needed it for the entry form, because without a properly filled in entry form, you couldn't enter. All the details about the competition had been in another issue of *Our Times* ages ago, but you had to buy this particular issue for the entry form.

When I'd first told the others about it, they'd all tried like mad to persuade me to enter a story I wrote ages ago, called *Sound Bites*, but I didn't think that it was much good, so I was going to write a new one. Then, when I'd told my English teacher about it, she'd encouraged as many people as possible who were thirteen to fifteen to enter. Hardly anyone was bothering, though, because they all thought there was no point as it was a national competition and they wouldn't stand a chance.

I'd brought the magazine to school to remind me to try to persuade Fen or Luce to enter it, too. The only trouble was, time was running out. The closing date for entries was in three days' time, but I knew I could write a story quickly once I got down to it. Before assembly I'd been chatting to the others about the competition and once again they'd all been on and on at me to enter *Sound Bites*, but I absolutely did *not* want to.

"Why don't you enter two stories – *Sound Bites* and your new one?" Luce had said with a big grin on her face. It was like she'd worked out how to predict the weather for two years ahead or something.

"You're not allowed to enter more than one story," Fen and Andy had chanted in unison.

Fen and Luce had both said they weren't going to bother entering because they'd left it too late, and the others weren't really the "story writing" sort.

And now it was the beginning of morning break and my magazine was definitely nowhere to be seen and I *knew* I'd put it in my bag that morning. I'd even shown it to Luce before assembly.

"Luce, you haven't taken that magazine out of my bag, have you?"

She was deep into a magazine of her own with that dreamy look in her eyes that I knew so well. She didn't hear me.

"Calling Lucy Edmunson, calling Lucy Edmunson," I said in a voice that sounded as though it was coming over a loud speaker. "Lucy Edmunson needed back on earth. Please come back to earth directly."

"Isn't he totally gorgeous?" she breathed, without taking her eyes off the page that was mesmerizing her.

"Totally," I agreed, without looking.

"It says here that he likes dark-skinned girls…"

"Luce," I interrupted, "did you take that magazine I had in my bag?"

"No, I did *not*," she protested, knitting her eyebrows together as only Luce can.

6

"Just asking," I told her with a friendly smile, but Luce wasn't happy. Not only did she have the wrong colouring for lover boy in her magazine, but she'd been accused of taking *my* magazine, and *I* had the cheek to have the right colouring for the object of her passion.

"Well, he wouldn't like Leah either, and that's got to be a first," she consoled herself thoughtfully, while I went off to find the others. They were all in Fen and Tash's tutor-group room.

"I don't suppose any of you have seen that magazine I brought into school this morning?"

They all shook their heads and said things like "Why? Have you lost it?" and "When did you last see it?" But there was something about the way they were reacting that wasn't ringing true. Tash, who hadn't been in on the conversation before assembly, asked me if it was something important.

"Yes, it's got the entry form in it for that writing competition. I can't enter unless I find it."

It was at this point that I noticed that Fen was looking really embarrassed. A ridiculous thought immediately crossed my mind, and once I'd thought it I couldn't get rid of it. It occurred to me that she might have taken the magazine so she could enter the competition herself, but obviously I couldn't accuse her just like that. If it was true, though, it was a pretty selfish thing to do. My mind was doing somersaults trying to work out what to say next.

"Um ... did you say you were going to enter the competition or not, Fen?" I asked, trying to sound as casual as possible.

"No. I've got too much to do with writing the play for Emmy's class." (Emmy is Fen's five-year-old sister, by the way.)

Now I was really stuck for words, especially as a little voice in my head was saying, *You're not telling the truth, Fen...*

"What subject have you got to write on?" Leah asked me.

"Any environmental issue."

"Oh, not that again," Andy said with a sigh. "Why can't these adults think of anything original for a change?"

"I expect they're looking to see who can make something original out of an unoriginal subject," Tash pointed out.

"Exactly," I agreed.

"Well, I still think you ought to send in the *Sound Bites* story. It's so brilliant, Jaimes," Fen said.

I shook my head and said, "There's no point in trying to persuade me because the answer is *no!* Anyway," I went on, changing the subject, "I can't work out why anyone would take the magazine unless it was for the entry form. It's a really boring magazine."

Nobody said anything, though they all looked sympathetic, but it wasn't until I was halfway back to my registration room that I stopped dead in my tracks as another horrible thought struck me.

What if it *was* Fen who had taken the magazine, and not just to get an entry form for herself, but to prevent me from entering? No, surely not. I frowned and told myself off for having horrible thoughts about one of my friends. Fen wouldn't sink so low as to deliberately take my magazine, would she?

"Lost your way, Jaimini?" someone called from behind me, interrupting my thoughts. It was Leoni Weston. She was with her friend Alex Drew. They're both year-eight girls, same as me, and they were grinning as though they'd just cracked the joke of the century.

I didn't bother to reply, just gave them a withering look and carried on walking. Actually, I don't think they particularly like me. I don't know why I think that but sometimes you just get a feeling, don't you?

Back in our registration room, I wandered over to the window, because Luce was nowhere to be seen. It was quite interesting observing the world going on without anyone being aware that they're being watched. Most people were in groups or pairs, but over to one side, standing by herself, was a girl called Evi Bligh. She hasn't been at our school very long, and apparently this is her eighth school because her dad's job means the family has to move a lot. It must be horrible to keep having to change schools. I'd hate it because you'd keep having to try and make new friends.

"Who are you gawping at?" Luce asked, joining me at the window.

"Actually, I was watching Evi. She's got no friends, has she?"

"No, I suppose she hasn't..." Luce replied. "But then it's not surprising, is it, seeing as she's not very nice."

With that, Luce wandered off, leaving me to my thoughts. Evi Bligh is in all the top sets like me but she's always the last person to have anyone sitting next to her. For some reason, she's just not very popular. Occasionally, I've sat next to her, but she never really says anything much to me and I've given up trying to be friendly when I don't get anything back.

Evi was leaning against the wall in her usual pose, biting her right thumbnail. Her school skirt is very long and her shirt always looks whiter than white. The thing that really stands out about her, though, is her shoes. They're too posh for school, somehow. They don't have heels or anything, but they're really slim and so shiny that they look navy blue, not black.

As I watched Evi, I witnessed something really appalling. Two boys walked past her and one of them looked round to check no one was watching, then the other one pushed her roughly so that she banged her head on the wall and nearly fell over. Then, calm as anything, the two boys said something to her, which obviously I couldn't hear, before strolling off.

If that had been me I would have rushed off to tell someone, or at least reacted in some way, like yelling at them or hitting them back or even by bursting into tears! But Evi just stood there as though being knocked about by a rough boy was the most normal thing in the world.

"Did you see that?" I asked Luce, feeling horrified at what I'd just witnessed.

"What?" she replied, but I could see she was back into her magazine again. I sat down beside her and told her exactly what I'd just seen.

"What are you going to do?" Luce asked me, wide-eyed.

We both answered her question together. "Report them."

"What are their names?" was Luce's next question.

"No idea," I replied. "I thought I recognized one of them but I couldn't be certain."

"Let's go and talk to Evi," Luce suggested, so we belted outside, but when we got to where she'd been standing, we found ourselves looking at a blank wall. Evi was nowhere to be seen, and then the bell went for the end of break so there was nothing Luce and I could do for a while.

We didn't see Evi again all day and decided we'd have to leave any action on our part till tomorrow. So, at a quarter to four, Luce, myself and all the others went off to the café. It was my turn to work and the others were just coming along to sit and have a drink of coke or something. We often do that after school, though it isn't often that all of us manage to go together, because sometimes one of us has a club or a rehearsal or practice or something after school.

"So, it's the brainy one today, is it?" Kevin, the chef, remarked with a big grin on his face as I walked through the back door into the kitchen. He'd recently found out what we call each other and he took great delight in using these names for us when we were at work.

"I wish you wouldn't call me that," I said, with a huge sigh.

"You should be proud to be the brainy one," he answered, putting two slices of bread into the wire toaster which goes on the Aga.

"Well, I'm *not* proud," I assured him, firmly.

"Hi, pet," said Jan, rushing in from the café.

12

"How are things?"

"Fine, apart from a missing magazine and a cheeky chef," I summarized quickly.

"Can't do much about the magazine but I'll sort the chef for you," and with that she pretended to stamp on Kevin's right foot, then rushed back into the café with a tray of orders.

"Jan's in a good mood," I commented, putting on a crisp white apron from the drawer.

"Well, if stamping on people's feet is what she does when she's in a good mood, I'd hate to meet her when she's in a bad one!" Kevin retorted. "Here you go, four pans and a couple of bowls."

"Hi, Jaimini," said Becky, coming in after a few minutes.

There's always one other person who's on duty at the same time as one of us, and it's either Becky or Mark. Becky is in her early twenties and is a very straightforward sort of person. She speaks her mind, if you know what I mean. She rarely chats with us, just quietly gets on with her work, though she does chat to the customers quite a bit. Kevin, by the way, is twenty-one and really nice. Luce thinks he's dishy, but then Luce thinks everyone's dishy!

I worked in the kitchen, washing up mainly, for at least a quarter of an hour, then went into the café with an order for table six. The moment I'd served that table I became aware of Luce frantically signalling to me to go over to her.

"Have you seen who's sitting in the corner? Evi! She's just come in," hissed Luce, clutching my arm as though she'd just spotted an adder and needed me to protect her. "Let's go and ask her who those boys were."

"What boys?" asked Fen.

"Tell you later," I replied, glancing round to check that it would be all right for me to stop work for a couple of minutes. Luce was already on her way, dragging me with her by the sleeve so I didn't exactly have much choice anyway.

"Evi," she said, plunging in with her usual conversational finesse, "Jaimini saw that boy push you at break time this morning. She just happened to be looking through the window ... and wondered..."

The reason Luce was trailing off was the look in Evi's eyes. She was sort of half frowning as though trying to work out what on earth Luce was on about. Luce looked to me for support.

"It's just that I felt really sorry for you and wanted to help out by reporting the boys, only I don't know their names..." I tried, but I was also feeling less and less sure of myself. Evi was still looking half puzzled and half – well, there's no other way of describing it – *completely* vacant.

"Evi, who are they?" Luce asked, tackling the subject head on.

"What are you talking about?" asked Evi, in her

strange voice that always sounded as though she'd lost it. (Her voice, I mean.)

Luce looked at me as if to say, Did you imagine the whole thing or something?

"It was you I saw, wasn't it?" I asked Evi slowly, even though I was double positive it had been her.

"I've no idea what you mean, honestly," Evi replied, lifting her shoulders and giving me an apologetic smile.

"But... I... Is it because you're scared you'll get into even more trouble if I report them?" I asked gently, while Luce nodded vigorously, as though that was her idea and I was merely the mouthpiece.

"I think you must have got me mixed up with someone else," Evi smiled, "because, you see, I never even went outside this morning. I stayed in at break time."

"Well... We only wanted to help..." Luce began to say, but I reckoned that it was about time we called it a day, because we were getting nowhere fast.

"Yeah, silly me, I obviously mistook you for someone else," I said, steering a rather indignant Luce away. "Seeya then, Evi."

"What's going on, Jaimes?" Luce whispered loudly the moment we were back with the others. "She's lying, she is. What did you drag me away for? I wanted to find out more."

15

"Because she's acting very mysteriously and obviously doesn't want us involved with whatever it is," I told her, which made the others all lean forwards and demand a blow by blow account of the great mystery.

"I've got to get back to work. Luce'll tell you," I said, glancing round at the café which was filling up rapidly.

"Luce'll exaggerate," Andy complained.

"*No* exaggeration, Luce!" I warned her, wagging my finger at her in mock heavy-adult-warning style.

"That's two mysteries in one day," Tash said, rubbing her hands with glee.

"What's the other one?" I heard Luce asking as I disappeared into the kitchen. It was only then that I realized I hadn't really tackled Luce properly over the missing magazine. I thought back to morning break and Fen's reaction when I'd mentioned the competition. As I loaded the dishwasher, peeled potatoes and buttered toast, I had an even worse thought. What if *Luce* had taken the magazine and she was only pretending to be engrossed in her own magazine as a front to stop me suspecting her? I began an argument in my head.

No, Luce wouldn't do that. She's your friend. Why should she, anyway?

Maybe for the same reason that Fen might.

Because she wants to enter the competition and she doesn't want you to enter.

That's ridiculous. There's absolutely nothing to suggest that either of them would do that.

Except that no one else would take the magazine, and it's true that they did both originally intend to enter the competition, and now Fen's changed her mind.

But Luce hasn't.

How do you know?

Er ... I don't.

So why don't you find out and if she says she is still entering it, and she's got her own entry form, then you'll know you were wrong to suspect her.

But what about Fen?

Forget about Fen. For goodness' sake. She's your friend as well. Friends don't behave like that.

By the time I'd finished the two-sided conversation in my head I felt rather ashamed of myself for ever suspecting Fen and Luce in the first place. I made the decision to report the missing magazine the very next day, but in the meantime I'd get one of the girls to nip up to the newsagent's before it closed and get me another copy, and I'd just have to pray that there *was* one there.

Feeling positive and sensible, I went back to the café and approached the table where Luce and the others were sitting.

"I don't suppose one of you could do me a big favour, could you?" I asked.

Tash was the first to say yes and asked me what it was.

"You know that magazine I lost, well, could you see if they've got another one at the news-agent's? It's called *Our Times*."

"I'll get you one," Fen immediately offered. "I promised I'd get a comic for Emmy. I'll go right now, in fact, then I can bring it back for you."

"Oh, it's OK, tomorrow will do," I assured her.

"I don't mind, honestly," she replied.

Then I turned to Luce.

"Are you still entering the competition, Luce?"

"No, I can't be bothered," she answered, casually.

"Oh, go on, Luce. You ought to," I tried to persuade her, mainly because I didn't want to go back to suspecting my friends again.

"No, I think I'll just stick to the cookery comp," she said. "I might stand a chance of getting some-where in that!"

I was about to protest, but decided against it because Jan was signalling to me to get some drinks for one of the other tables, so I went over to the counter and started making milkshakes and cappuccinos, but my mind was on other things. I saw Fen leave the café, then I watched for a few seconds as Luce talked very excitedly to Tash, and guessed she was telling her about her entry for the cookery competition.

This competition was one of Kevin's brain-waves. He has a friend called Martin Rhuanna who's also a chef and has even been on television once. Kevin said he could get Martin to come along and judge a cookery competition for under-eighteens, right here in the café. Jan had thought that this was a brilliant idea and a great customer puller, so she'd put an advert in the local paper telling people to get details and entry forms from the café.

So far it was proving very popular. The first round had already taken place, and for that, Martin had had to visit four different schools where loads of people had made dishes in their cookery lessons. Martin got to taste every single dish, and also took away with him a piece of paper from every competitor. On the paper the com-petitors had to write out the recipe for their dish and say what they would serve with it, and also say what the rest of the meal would be. It meant quite a lot of work for Martin.

Luce had already done that part of the com-petition and she was waiting to hear whether or not she'd got through to the final, but as there were only going to be three finalists, it would be pretty tough.

I wasn't interested in entering because cookery

isn't really my thing, but Luce was very keen, and she'd seen a photo of Martin Rhuanna which had made her even keener to enter because he was very good-looking indeed.

I was so engrossed in my thoughts that one of the milkshakes I was making frothed out all over the place and I accidentally knocked over the other one. Goodness knows how! All I know is that I was really cross with myself for being so clumsy, and Jan gave me a very funny look. So for the next twenty minutes I focused totally on what I was doing, earning myself at least two complimentary smiles from Jan, which made me feel better.

I'd completely forgotten about the story competition and the magazine and everything until Fen reappeared when I was clearing one of the tables.

"I'm afraid they didn't have any more copies of *Our Times*," she said, looking sympathetic.

"Oh well, never mind," I said, trying not to show my disappointment. "I expect my old one'll turn up. I'm going to report it missing tomorrow."

"Yeah, I expect it will," she replied. "See you tomorrow, then." Then off she went. The others had all left about ten minutes before.

The rest of my duty went without anything eventful happening and at six o'clock I set off for home. For some unknown reason, I decided to go past the newsagent's, even though it meant going out of my way. I've no idea why I did that. The newsagent's was closed, of course, but I glanced in at the window anyway, and there in the centre was a copy of *Our Times*. An involuntary shiver passed through me and my mouth felt dry.

Why had Fen said there weren't any copies? My spirits sank because I knew now that I had been right to suspect her. But what could I do? What could I say? Should I have a word with Tash? No, I couldn't possibly. Fen was her best friend, and Tash couldn't bear it when there was friction between people. Maybe I'd speak to Luce. But then, I wasn't even sure about what Luce was up to, was I? What about Leah or Andy? No, I couldn't drag them into it. That would be stirring. I'd just have to make sure I asked Mum to buy the magazine first thing the next day, then forget about everything else.

After another big sigh I made my way quickly home, all the way working on the plot of the story I was going to write. I was finding it very difficult to concentrate, though, because I kept picturing that strange vacant expression on Evi Bligh's face.

Chapter 2

The next morning I set my alarm to go off at a quarter to six because I wanted to have breakfast with Mum and Dad. We don't normally get up that early in our family, but on this particular day, Dad was going away for two or three days and I wanted to see him before he went. I'd spent the whole of the previous evening working in my room on my story and it was all finished. I'd printed it out on our computer and was really pleased with it – even fairly hopeful – though I knew it wasn't a good idea to feel too optimistic because that would only make the disappointment unbearable if I didn't get anywhere. I was clutching the story right there and then at the breakfast table because I didn't want to let it out of my sight in case anything happened to it.

"You won't forget to get that *Our Times* magazine, will you, Mum?" I said for about the tenth time.

"I won't forget, no, but I only hope it's still there, because these ante-natal clinic sessions sometimes run very late, you know."

I nodded and felt myself tensing up again. I had a bad feeling about this competition. Nothing was going right so far, which didn't bode well for the success of my story. If only the newsagent's was on the way to school, then I could get the magazine myself, but it wasn't, and I'd make myself late if I did a detour.

Mum is pregnant, by the way. It's so wonderful, because she's been trying to get pregnant for eleven whole years and had almost given up hope. I am an only child but I can't wait to have a brother or sister. When you're pregnant you have to go to regular check-ups at ante-natal clinics, and that's where Mum was going this morning.

"Can I read your story?" Dad asked, giving me a very searching look. Dad is a man of few words, which can make him seem a little hostile at times, but he isn't really. He's probably the second strictest father of all our fathers, after Andy's, but I respect him for his intelligence and his standards, even though he's sometimes made things quite difficult for me.

I felt flattered that he wanted to read my story, but I also felt anxious in case he thought it was rubbish. I handed it straight over and sat there tensely nibbling bits of toast while he read it. His expression didn't change at all as he was reading so I didn't have any clues as to whether he thought it was good, bad or so-so. When he'd finished he put it down slowly and looked at me.

"Wh ... what do you think?" I asked in a quivery voice.

"Very good," he said, breaking into a smile. "I think it's very good. Great idea for a plot, good characterization..."

I could just feel that there was a big "but" coming, and I could also feel my spirits sinking fast.

"But what, Dad?"

"No... It's fine, really."

"Please tell me..."

"Well, if I'm completely honest, I felt that there was something missing, but I don't know what that magic ingredient is..."

He must have seen the disappointment in my eyes, because he smiled again and said, "Don't listen to me. I'm probably talking rubbish. *I* couldn't have written anything half as good as that, you know."

With that he gulped down his last drop of coffee and went off to get ready for his business trip. Mum smiled at me.

"I don't suppose I can read it, can I?"

"Of course you can, Mum," I quickly assured her, feeling guilty because I hadn't asked her before, so when Dad had gone off on his trip, I stayed with Mum and read it over her shoulder. I'd called it *Making Waves* and I was really pleased with my opening sentence, which went like this...

When the noise finally stopped, it shocked Mr Zeta so much that he dropped the glass he was holding so it shattered into hundreds of tiny pieces, and made its own small impact on the silence.

I cleared away the breakfast dishes after that, leaving Mum to read the rest of the story on her own. She never did get to the end of it, though, because she suddenly gripped the kitchen table and made a noise as if she was in great pain. She bent over, hunching her shoulders, but I saw her face and there was as much fear as pain in her expression.

"What is it, Mum? What's happened?" I asked, rushing over to her and putting my arm round her.

"I don't know," she replied after a few seconds. "I think something may be happening to the baby..."

I gasped and looked round the kitchen in a panic. I don't know what on earth I was looking for.

"What shall I do? Shall I telephone the doctor?"

"I'm going up to bed, Jaimini. It's a bit early to

phone the doctor. Leave it half an hour, then phone him."

I helped Mum upstairs, then went back down again and sat at the kitchen table wondering whether I ought to try praying. I didn't think that would do any good as I'd never really done it before, and I had the feeling that God might not be all that interested in people who only prayed when they wanted something. I felt close to tears. If Mum had a miscarriage, it seemed to me that our whole family would go into mourning for ever. We'd all waited so long for this baby.

In the end I phoned the doctor before half an hour had passed because I couldn't bear to wait any longer. There was an answerphone message telling me the number to ring for the doctor in an emergency. I phoned that number and Dr Wood answered. She didn't say much on the phone, just listened carefully and asked me one or two questions, then took directions to our house and said she'd be there in about an hour.

I went up to Mum and told her what the doctor had said, and she just nodded. "Can I get you anything, Mum?"

She shook her head and a tear rolled down her face. "Oh, Mum…" I said, rushing over to give her another hug. "Do you think you're…?"

I couldn't say the word *miscarrying*. I just couldn't say it. It was too harsh, and there was something inside me that thought if I didn't say it, it wouldn't happen.

She just nodded again and I assured her I'd stay with her till the doctor came, and take the day off school if she wanted me to. As I was saying this I suddenly remembered about the magazine. I would have to go and buy it myself now Mum wasn't well. "Oh, come on, Doctor Wood! Hurry up, please, and please stop Mum from losing this baby…" That was the nearest I got to praying.

It was almost half-past nine when Doctor Wood arrived, full of apologies, and smiling away as though she was visiting an old lady who needed cheering up or something. She stayed with Mum for forty minutes and every minute of that time was agony. I felt as though I was in Limboland. There was absolutely nothing I could do, no one I could phone, nowhere I could go. I was dying to know if Mum and the baby were going to be all right, and I was beginning to feel a bit desperate about getting to the newsagent's in time to buy *Our Times* before someone else did.

The second I heard the door opening upstairs I was in the hall, standing like a ramrod, my eyes ready to clamp on to the doctor's so I could judge instantly how serious things were. When her eyes met mine I saw straight away that it *was* serious, but she immediately smiled and tried to look unconcerned.

"Your mum's going into hospital tomorrow for a stitch…" she explained as she came downstairs. "Don't look so worried. It's quite common…" She had reached the bottom of the stairs and she put an arm round my shoulders. "You should be at school, shouldn't you? Is there anyone who could come in and look after your mum for a while?"

"I'm not sure…" I began, because I didn't think Mum would want anyone looking after her. The doctor was frowning and I didn't want her to send in a complete stranger or something, so I pretended I'd just thought of the perfect person.

"Oh yes, Mrs Smith. She could come, I'm sure."

This had the instant effect of making Dr Wood relax into a smile and make for the front door. As I was shutting the door I thought how easily some grown ups are taken in. I mean – Mrs Smith – it's not exactly the most original name in the world, is it? I rushed upstairs and went in to see Mum.

"That was quite a scare, wasn't it?" she smiled weakly.

"Are you going to be all right, Mum?" I asked, feeling a tiny bit relieved because Mum looked less worried now.

"I hope so, love. I've got to go into hospital tomorrow but I'll be back the next day. I wondered if it might be best for you to stay at

28

Luce's as Dad isn't here... I mean, I could contact him and ask him to come home, of course, but it seems ridiculous when there's absolutely nothing he can do."

"But he'll *want* to come home when you tell him what's happened... I presume he'll phone this evening, won't he?"

"Yes, he said he would." Mum bit her lip and I knew exactly what was coming. "I've decided not to tell him there's a problem, love. It's not exactly lying because it's just leaving something out. Only I think he'll be so worried, and no matter how much I assure him that there's nothing he can do if he turns round and comes all the way back, he'll still want to do it anyway."

"But if anything goes wrong, Dad would feel terrible if he wasn't there with you."

"It can't go wrong before he gets back," Mum said, patting my hand absentmindedly. This proved to me that she wasn't a hundred per cent sure of what she was saying because she would never normally pat my hand like that.

I was about to tell her I'd decided to take the day off school when she suddenly said, "Look, why don't you go to school now? I'm going to give Mrs Danin a ring. She'll pop in from time to time, I'm sure."

I'd forgotten all about Mrs Danin. She was our next-door neighbour and was in her fifties with two grown-up children who lived miles away. Even though we'd lived next door to her for ages, we didn't really know her all that well, but she always said hello and asked me how things were going at school. When I was little she used to babysit for me when Mum and Dad went out.

As soon as Mum had phoned Mrs Danin and I was sure that she was going to be all right, I agreed to go to school. I had planned to go the long way round so that I could call in at the newsagent's on the way. So I settled Mum down with a cup of tea and a flask for later, a book and two magazines, then went downstairs and out of the front door calling out "Bye Mum, love you, see you soon, take care, won't be long, don't be sad, bye, byeeee…"

I don't know at what point during the walk to the newsagent's I switched from thinking about Mum to thinking about the competition, but I was deep into analysing every word that Dad had said about my story by the time I got within fifty paces of the newsagent's. My heart was beating faster than usual because I was so worried in case the magazine wasn't there. It must be, I figured. It couldn't be all that popular.

Of course, that got me thinking about Fen. She'd deliberately lied to me about the magazine. I knew that Fen was ambitious, of course, and we all knew that she wanted to be a writer when she grew up, but I never thought in a million years that she would go to these lengths to make sure that I didn't stand in the way of her winning the competition. The more I thought about it, the more she made me sick.

I had reached the newsagent's without even realizing it, and there, coming out of the shop right in front of me, was Luce's mum, Melanie.

"Hello, Jaimini! This is a surprise!"

"Mum's had to go to bed because she thought she was beginning to miscarry…"

"Oh no!" Melanie said, putting her hand to her cheek and looking very wide-eyed.

"The doctor's been to see her this morning and she's got to go into hospital tomorrow to have a stitch."

"Oh, Jaimini, I'm so sorry to hear that," said Melanie, sounding close to tears. "Has she got someone with her? Shall I pop in and see her?"

"It's all right, she's got Mrs Danin on the other end of the phone…" I was on the point of saying, *Dad's away, you see, and Mum was wondering whether I could spend tomorrow night at your place*, when I suddenly noticed what Melanie had in her hand – a copy of *Our Times*. My eyes slid to the window behind her and I saw that there was now no copy in the window. For a second I was speechless, as loads of possible things to say whizzed in and out of my brain like a line of crazy

31

divers going off a cliff and disappearing from view.

Why have you bought that magazine, Melanie?

Luce told you to get that magazine, didn't she?

Can I borrow that magazine, Melanie?

Could I possibly take one page out of that magazine?

"I'll give her a ring when I get home," Melanie was saying, but I still wasn't capable of speech, so I made a noise that could have been "OK" at a pinch, then started to go. She looked at me sympathetically and patted my arm, telling me not to worry, then she went off. I walked very slowly for twenty paces, then turned round, checked she was nowhere in sight, and rushed back to the newsagent's and went in.

"Have you got a copy of *Our Times*, please?" I asked breathlessly.

"Sorry, just sold the last one. Can I help you?"

The shop assistant had already turned to the next customer, so I walked out feeling totally miserable, and made my way very slowly to school. I actually considered turning round and going back home, because I did *not* want to see Luce *or* Fen. They were both acting really selfishly. If I'd been a brave sort of person like Andy, I'd come right out with what I was thinking and say, "Look, I know what you're both doing and I think you're pathetic." It sounded so easy, so why didn't I do it?

The answer was that I couldn't be absolutely sure I *was* right, and I'd look utterly stupid if there was some perfectly reasonable explanation for their behaviour. The other reason I didn't want to confront them was because I'm a bit like Tash in that respect: I don't like it when people aren't friends. I suppose I'm just weak, but I'd rather ignore things than make waves. I've always been like that. The truth is, that no matter how much the others have always treated me totally like one of them, I've always felt, in some small way, that I don't really belong. It's difficult to explain, but it's to do with the colour of my skin.

When I got to school it was the middle of morning break. I guessed the others would be down on the netball courts which is where we always go when it's fine. The netball courts are miles from everywhere else so it's a good place for having private conversations. I didn't go down there, partly because of not wanting to see Fen or Luce, but mainly because I wanted to show Mrs Merle my story.

Mrs Merle was actually the music teacher and she also taught some PSE but she was easily my favourite teacher and I trusted her opinion more than any other teacher's. I knocked on the staff-room door and it was Mrs Crowhurst who answered. Mrs Crowhurst is Luce's English teacher. Her eyes went straight to what I had in my hand.

"Someone else entering the literary competition, I see," she commented with the nearest she ever got to a smile appearing briefly on her face. As you may have gathered, I am not a great fan of Mrs Crowhurst's.

"Why? Who else is entering?" I quickly asked before I could change my mind.

"Half the school, as far as I can tell," she answered, which didn't tell me what I wanted to know, but there was no way I could say *Does that include Lucy Edmunson and Fenella Brooks?* because she'd wonder why I didn't ask them myself.

"Is Mrs Merle there, please?" I asked instead.

She didn't even answer me, just turned round and called out to Mrs Merle. I bet she'd thought at first that I'd come to show *her* my story, and wasn't too happy to find out that I'd actually come to show it to Mrs Merle. I've often noticed that the teachers who aren't very nice are always jealous of the ones who are.

"Hello, Jaimini. What can I do for you?" said Mrs Merle, who always looked so pleased to see anyone, no matter how busy she was.

"I was wondering if you'd look at my story. It's for the competition. You may think I could improve it."

"I'm sure I won't, but yes, certainly, I'll take a look at it and I'll give it back to you after lunch. All right?"

"Yes, thank you ... and, the thing is, I seem to have lost my copy of the magazine with the entry form in it. I don't suppose you know if any of the teachers have got a spare one, do you?"

"They haven't, I'm afraid, because someone else was asking that yesterday. Oh dear, Jaimini. Have you really looked absolutely everywhere for your copy?"

"I'll go and double check," I told her, feeling more and more despondent with every passing minute.

There was nobody in my registration room at all. Luce's school bag was hanging on her chair and before I knew it I was rifling through it. I searched every inch of that bag but there was no magazine and no entry form to be seen. I was just weighing up whether I'd got time to go along to Fen's registration room and look through her bag before the end of break, when I looked on the desk where I usually sat for registration and there, as large as life, was my original magazine. I knew it was mine because Luce had coloured in the eyebrows of the woman on the front cover in black, and also blacked out one of her teeth. I flipped quickly to the page with the entry form and got the shock of my life to find that the page

35

had been very neatly and carefully cut out. I actually gasped in disbelief, and the bell went at that moment.

Without hanging about for even a second I went straight off to double maths with Mr Waring. None of the others were in my maths set, thank goodness, so I had time to think what to do. By the time the maths lesson was over I had decided that I would *have* to say something to Luce. She was supposed to be my best friend, for goodness' sake, and yet there was all this rivalry and nastiness going on between us.

I went straight off to find Luce at lunch time, but she was nowhere to be seen. I did come across Fen, though, who was with Tash in the dinner queue. I guessed Andy would be at a sports practice and Leah at orchestra, but goodness only knew where Luce had got to.

"Luce had to go to the nurse. She's not feeling well," Tash said, as I approached her and Fen in the queue. "Where were you this morning?" she went on to ask.

"Mum's in bed. She had some pains and she's bleeding," I explained softly.

"Oh, Jaimes," said Tash, putting her arm round my shoulder.

"Oh, your poor mum," Fen added. They both looked so sympathetic. I couldn't believe I ever mistrusted Fen. I knew I had to say something about the competition, though, before I changed my mind, and if I couldn't say it to Luce I'd have to say it to Fen. What I should have done was jump right in and ask her why she told me there were no copies of *Our Times* left in the newsagent's when there was one on display right in the middle of the window. Of course, being me, I went for the softer option. I took a deep breath.

"Are you really not entering the competition, Fen?" I asked, looking straight into her eyes.

"Yes, I told you," she said, sounding and looking totally convincing.

"What about Luce?" I went on.

"Er ... I don't think she is, either," Fen replied, only this time she definitely looked embarrassed and Tash had even looked away, which made me very suspicious.

"I haven't got a form to fill in, now," I said softly.

Tash's eyes flew back to my face. I knew that that would make her sympathetic. It was impossible to tell from the look on Fen's face *what* she was thinking.

"Which story are you entering, Jaimini?" she asked, casually.

"One I wrote last night," I told her a bit sharply. "Only I don't know if I *can* enter it, do I?"

At that moment Mrs Merle suddenly appeared behind me.

"I've read your story, and I think it's excellent, Jaimini," she told me warmly. "*And*, even better, I've found a spare entry form, so I've filled it in for you and even put it in an envelope. How's that for good service, eh?"

She was practically laughing and so was I. This was definitely the happiest moment of my day. It looked as though everything was going to turn out all right, after all. I noticed a look pass between Fen and Tash, but I couldn't work out what the look said, so I ignored it because I didn't care now that my guardian angel, Mrs Merle, had sorted everything out for me.

"Let me at least pay for the stamp," I said, rootling around in my bag for my purse.

"If you insist," said Mrs Merle, seeing that she had no choice because I'd thrust fifty pence into her hand.

"When are the results coming out?" I asked her.

"Four weeks today," Fen said. Mrs Merle and I turned shocked expressions on her. My shock was because Fen knew the answer to that question when she apparently wasn't even entering.

"My goodness! That must be the fastest judged competition in history!" said Mrs Merle, which explained why she had appeared shocked. "Have you entered a story yourself, Fen?"

"No, I haven't actually," Fen said. "I've been

quite busy, you see… I'm writing the play for my sister's class at primary school."

If anything I was more in the dark now I'd "confronted" Fen. Something wasn't adding up, but, as I've already said, I don't like making waves and especially not with Tash's best friend, so I decided that I'd just try and forget about the newsagent's episode, now that my story was safely on its way. And as for Luce, I'd try and trust her too, though that wouldn't be so easy. There were too many pictures that I didn't like in my head – Melanie holding that magazine, my own magazine with the missing page, and that look that had passed between Fen and Tash when they realized that my story was all ready to go, entry form and all!

And where was Luce? Seeing the nurse. Huh! She was avoiding me, that's what she was doing.

Well, two could play at that game.

Chapter 3

I felt pretty callous not going to see Luce, but on the other hand this was the perfect way of showing her that I was not impressed with the way she was carrying on at the moment. I'd asked Tash what was the matter with her and she didn't sound all that concerned, so if even Tash wasn't particularly bothered I knew I had no reason to feel too guilty. Apparently Luce just had a headache.

At the end of school I walked down to the café with Leah and Andy. They told me that Luce had gone home during the afternoon. I decided not to say anything more to anyone about the competition, but I *did* tell Leah and Andy about Mum, and they were both really sympathetic.

Fen was on duty, so Tash, Leah, Andy and I all sat down together at a table for four. Mark appeared in no time at all and took our order.

Either Mark or Becky takes over after lunch when Debra goes home. Debra's the one person who works at the café who we rarely see, because she works from nine o'clock till three o'clock Monday to Friday.

Mark is seventeen and very nice. He's like a gentle giant. He's studying the Martial Arts and just works at the café for a bit of extra money. He also earns money teaching judo.

"So what's it to be today, girls? Coke on the rocks? Lemonade shaken but not stirred?" He waited, pen poised over his pad, imitating the type of waiter you'd find in a very posh restaurant or hotel. We all wanted chocolate milkshakes as it happened.

After about a quarter of an hour, Tash's brother Danny appeared with their little sister, Peta. He didn't look very pleased. Danny is fifteen and doesn't look at all like Tash. He's got blond floppy hair and is tall and quite athletic-looking. He's going out with Leah's sister, Kim, who is also fifteen.

"Oh, sorry, Dan!" Tash said, clapping her hand to her mouth. "I forgot! Sorry."

Danny pursed his lips, gave Tash a withering look, said hi to Leah, then disappeared, leaving Peta standing on her own in the middle of the café.

"I was supposed to be looking after Peta after

school so that Danny could get on with revision for his exams. Mum's out at work, you see," explained Tash, looking rather pink.

Peta, who is just three and very entertaining – though Tash doesn't always agree – had scrambled up on to the nearest chair and was shouting across the café at Fen.

"Hi, Fenny Penny! Look, it's me! Peta! I'm on vis chair waving to you."

Jan swung round and looked as though she was about to blow a fuse, but because the general atmosphere in the café was a good one, with everybody looking on in amusement at Peta's little outburst, she soon relaxed, but gave Tash a look that said, *So far so good, but don't let this get out of hand.*

"Get down, Peta, and come and sit with us," said Tash firmly but quietly. Peta looked as though she was about to protest but then changed her mind because Tash had deliberately thrown a glance over at all the cakes, then given Peta a sort of secretive smile. Peta nodded her head vigorously with big, excited eyes, so off they went so she could choose a cake. Tash is no fool!

Peta had chosen the biggest slice of cherry cake you ever saw, and was having a great time breaking off tiny bits and crumbling them up, then trying to scoop them on to her little fork and get them to her wide open mouth without letting any drop. If she let even one crumb fall, she started all over again. As you can imagine, this kept her occupied for ages while the rest of us chatted away about everything except literary competitions.

We were in the middle of discussing spot removing creams when I suddenly noticed Evi Bligh sitting at a table quite near the door, all on her own. She was eating a slice of the same cake that Peta was eating and seemed equally absorbed in it. I thought of asking if she wanted to sit with us, but remembering how non-communicative she'd been the previous day, I quickly abandoned that idea. Looking round, I also realized that Leoni Weston and Alex Drew were in the café, deep in conversation at a table for two.

Our own conversation moved on to hair products and I came in for a lot of compliments on my hair.

"Why is your hair always so shiny?" complained Leah. "My hair just looks sort of flat."

"It must take hours to wash your hair, you two," Andy said, with a grin.

"Well, I'd love to have hair as short as yours," said Leah, "but I'd look absolutely stupid, I know." Then she produced a photo from her bag of someone with shoulder-length hair, and said she was thinking of having hers cut off to look like the girl in the picture.

We crowded round to look at the photo and were so absorbed that we didn't notice Peta's absence, until Andy suddenly jumped up and stared at the door with a horrified expression on her face. All our eyes instantly followed her gaze, and Tash cried out as though she was in agony, "Peta!"

Little Peta was outside the café standing on the edge of the pavement and about to step into the road. I felt sick. Andy plunged to the door as fast as she could, but Evi Bligh, who was nearer, took in the situation at a glance and, with great presence of mind, flung open the door, crashed outside, scooped Peta up when she was two steps into the road and saved her life, because a Range Rover went by a moment later, and judging by its speed it would never have been able to stop in time.

I was trembling so much I had to sit down, so what Tash must have felt like I don't know. She was crying with relief when she took her little sister out of Evi's arms and sat down with her, rocking her and holding her tight. Peta looked shocked too, mainly, I think, because her sister was crying and everybody else looked so stunned, and she probably didn't really understand why, except that it was to do with her.

The whole café seemed to be glued to the action at our table. The rest of us were all crowding round and telling Tash it wasn't her

44

fault, but Tash was shaking her head and insisting that it was. She kept on and on about what a hopeless big sister she was, and how if it hadn't been for Evi...

At that point we all realized that poor Evi, who had been the heroine in all this, was sitting back on her own again at her table. Tash beckoned to her to come and join us, and Evi smiled and drew up a chair. I noticed Peta was scowling at her, but didn't really think any more about that just then.

"I don't know how to thank you," said Tash softly, through her last lingering tears.

"Oh, I didn't do any more than anyone else would have done," Evi said, modestly.

"You won't ever go out of the café, or any building, on your own again, will you, Peta?" said Tash, turning Peta's face to look at her properly so that she realized how important it was.

"I wasn't going to go out," Peta replied earnestly, looking back at Tash.

"But you *did* go out, and that's not allowed, Peta. You won't ever do it again, will you?"

"She put me out," said Peta, pointing at Evi but keeping her eyes on Tash.

"No," smiled Tash. "Evi got you back in safely, otherwise a big car might have knocked you down. It's very dangerous on the road."

At that point Jan appeared and bent down beside Tash.

"I gather you've had some drama over here," she said, sympathetically. She obviously realized that Tash didn't need anyone telling her off or being cross with her right at that moment.

"If it hadn't been for Evi..." Tash began, but she couldn't finish her sentence. She dissolved into tears again.

Jan mouthed *Well done!* at Evi and gave her a nice smile, then went back to work, knowing that Tash would recover more quickly without adults around.

"But, I'm telling you, *she* made me go out," insisted Peta in a high-pitched squeak.

Evi went a bit red and I felt quite sorry for her just then.

"She must be getting confused, I think," she offered, quietly. "You see, when Leoni and Alex were going, they left the door open for a bit while they finished their conversation. I didn't see Peta at that moment, but I'm surprised *they* didn't see her because she must have been right by the door... You don't think...? No ... it's OK."

"What?" we all asked at the same time.

"No, nothing. It was a ridiculous thought, forget it."

When people say that, it only makes you all the more keen to find out what they were going to say, so naturally we all pressed Evi to go on.

"It's just that I can't see how they could have

failed to see Peta standing there... I mean, it's almost as though they did it on..."

"On purpose, you mean?" Andy breathed slowly.

Evi looked down, and the rest of us stayed silent and wide-eyed as we considered this awful thought.

"They'd never do that ... would they?" asked Tash, very softly.

"No ... they'd have no reason to do a thing like that," agreed Leah, equally softly.

Still Evi just looked down.

"Do you know something that we don't?" I asked Evi, beginning to feel the stirrings of suspicion.

"No... It's just that I don't see how they could have failed to realize that little Peta was there."

Still nobody said anything, but then we gradually started talking again, and things began to get back to normal.

After another few minutes we all decided to go home. Evi said she'd walk with Tash and Peta, because apparently she lived quite near Tash's house. I was the last one out of the door and just as I was shutting it behind me, Fen came rushing out of the kitchen gesticulating wildly at me. I wondered what on earth she was trying to say.

"There's been a phone call from a Mrs Danin. Your mum has got to go into hospital this afternoon after all, because everything's getting a bit more urgent, apparently. The ambulance is going to pick her up in about a quarter of an hour, so Mrs Danin says can you get home quickly?"

"I'm on my way," I said as I rushed out and hurtled past the others, calling out, "Mum's going into hospital!"

"Oh, good luck, Jaimes! Hope everything's OK," called Tash.

"Yeah, good luck!" the others all said, and if they said anything else I didn't hear it, because I was running so fast to try and get back in time to see Mum. I really wanted to go to hospital with her, so she wouldn't be all on her own.

When I got home, the ambulance was outside and the ambulance men were just helping Mum in. I rushed inside after her and gave her a big hug.

"What's happened, Mum? Why is it more urgent?"

"Don't worry, love, the hospital have just managed to find a bed for me today rather than having to wait till tomorrow, so the sooner I get into hospital, the sooner they can do the stitch and the better the chances of everything being all right."

I could tell Mum was trying to be brave and it just made me feel all the more sad.

"Can I come too, Mum? Pleeeease?"

"No, love, you can't. Look, I want you to stay the night at Luce's. I've phoned Melanie and she says that's fine."

"But Luce is ill, Mum. Can't I stay with one of the others?"

"No, love. I've organized it with Melanie. She told me that Luce had been a bit under the weather at school but apparently she seems much better now, so pack a bag and go straight over there. I'll be back tomorrow. It's just for tonight, all right?"

"Yes, all right, Mum."

The ambulance men were all ready to go. It was only me who was stopping them from going.

"Hope you're better after the operation, Mum. Love you."

"Love you, too. And *don't* worry. I'll be fine."

She smiled weakly at me and I felt a lump in my throat because she was still just being brave.

Waving the ambulance off made me feel sadder still, but the moment it had gone I began to think about that night and what I was going to do. There was no way I was going to stay at Luce's. She'd obviously just been pretending to be ill in the afternoon, because she was too embarrassed to face me. Let's face it, we weren't even friends. At least *I* wasn't friends with her. I'd rather spend the night with anyone other than Luce, but what could I do? Mum had arranged it all.

It wouldn't actually be a problem – as far as Mum was concerned – if I stayed with Leah or Tash or even Andy, but the problem was Luce. She obviously knew I was supposed to be staying with her. It would just make things between us even worse if she found out that I'd stayed with one of the others. And also the others might think it rather strange if I wanted to stay with them in preference to Luce. They'd want to know what was going on, and it was all too complicated to explain.

I sat down on the doorstep with my elbows on my knees and my chin cupped in my hands and thought hard. After about ten seconds of staring into space, a great idea came to me. I wouldn't stay with anyone. I'd stay at home on my own. I'd phone up and make some excuse to Melanie. I could say that Mrs Danin was going to spend the night with me at home. After all, Melanie would never find out that she hadn't. And even if she *did* find out, it wouldn't be for ages, and by then I'd just tell Mum the truth and tell her exactly why. She wouldn't be cross because she'd be so wrapped up in the baby...

The baby! *Oh, please let the stitch work! Please don't let us lose this baby!*

As I'd been staring at the ground, totally en-grossed in my thoughts, I had crossed my fingers without realizing, and then I'd crossed my legs, and my arms as well, so you could imagine I felt really silly when I looked up to see Tash standing there clutching Peta's hand, and on the other side of Peta, holding her other hand, was Evi Bligh.

"Hi, Jaimini! What are you doing?" Tash said, with a giggle.

"Thinking about Mum. I'm crossing every part of my body, because I don't want anything to happen to the baby."

I was on the point of asking what on earth she was doing at my house with Evi still in tow, but Tash, being so unselfish, wanted to check up on me before talking about herself.

"Is your mum still in bed?" she asked.

"No, she's gone into hospital…"

Oh, sugar! I'm *so* stupid. I'd only just decided not to tell a soul about my plan, and in two seconds flat I'd gone and spoilt it.

"Where are you staying tonight?" Tash asked immediately. "Because your dad's away, isn't he? You can stay at our place if you want, you know. Mum wouldn't mind, I'm certain."

My brain was doing overtime, trying to think whether or not this would be possible. What would I say to Melanie? That was the problem. Or *was* that the problem? I'd still have the problem of what to say to Melanie, even if I decided to stay on my own. No, the real problem was Luce. It was true I was cross with her and I did *not* want to spend the night at her place, but, on the other hand, I didn't want to drag Tash into our argument by staying the night at *her* place and making Luce upset or jealous.

Evi had moved a little distance away and was helping Peta pick daisies on our front lawn, and because it was just me and Tash, I decided to confide in her. It seemed the easiest thing to do, but I didn't particularly want Evi hearing because I didn't really know her or anything, and this was personal.

"The thing is, Tash, I'm not really friends with Luce at the moment, only Mum doesn't know that, and she's arranged for me to stay at Luce's tonight, but I absolutely don't want to. I'd love to stay at your place but that would only drag you into all this, which isn't fair..."

"So what are you going to do?"

It was typical of Tash that she didn't start getting cross with me, or quizzing me on what was wrong between Luce and me. She just got straight to the point.

"I'm going to stay here on my own."

Tash gasped and looked instantly worried. "Aren't you scared?"

"No, not really ... well, only a bit. I'll be all right when I fall asleep."

"But what if something happens during the night?"

52

"Like what?"

"Like a burglar or something!"

"Well, nobody will know I'm on my own, will they?"

"I suppose not... But what will you say to Luce's mum?"

"I'll say that it's OK because Dad came home."

I saw that Evi was coming nearer so I frowned at Tash and shook my head very subtly to tell her I didn't want to carry on talking about this in front of Evi.

"So, what are you lot doing here anyway?" I asked brightly, to change the subject.

"I was worried about you when you went belting off like that from the café, and I wanted to come and check you were OK."

Evi was standing right next to Tash by this time. I could tell Tash was feeling a bit crowded but was too nice to say so, especially since it was Evi who had rescued Peta from what could have been a terrible accident.

"And ... er ... Evi decided to come along, too," Tash finished rather lamely.

"Look what Peta's made for her big sister," Evi said, giving Peta an encouraging smile. Peta drew her hands from behind her back and held out a beautiful long daisy chain to Tash.

"Oh, it's lovely..."

Tash was on the point of taking it, when Peta

suddenly snatched it back and screwing up her eyes as though she couldn't bear to look, she crushed the daisies very fiercely, then dropped them and ground them into the gravel of our front drive, while we three looked on in horror.

"What did you do that for?" Tash asked incredulously.

In answer, Peta hurled herself up into Tash's arms and buried her head in her shoulder. She didn't cry. She didn't make a single sound, but her little back curled right over as though she couldn't get close enough.

"She's still upset after you-know-what," whispered Evi.

Tash nodded over Peta's head, and I thought how sensitive and understanding Evi was. She suddenly looked at her watch and said, "Oh dear, I'd better be getting back home. Come on, Peta, come and take my hand."

"I'm cuddling Tasha," came the muffled reply.

"But you're far too heavy for poor Tash," said Evi in a bright voice.

"I'm OK, honestly," Tash was quick to assure Evi. "Don't worry about us. You go, Evi ... and thanks again for what you did."

"It was nothing, and anyway I've got to go in your direction to get home, so I'll help you with Peta."

Tash was far too nice to tell Evi that she wanted

to be on her own with Peta, but I knew Tash, and I was sure she was wishing that Evi would just go.

With a small sigh, that only I detected, she gently put Peta down and set off home.

"See you tomorrow, Jaimini."

"Yeah, see you Tash. Bye, Evi. Bye, Peta."

"Take care," Tash added in a very soft voice.

I nodded and turned to go inside. I knew what she meant by that. She meant take care in that house all on my own.

As soon as I got inside I made myself go straight to the phone before I could change my mind.

"Hello, Melanie. It's Jaimini. I thought I'd better phone you because Dad's just turned up, so I won't need to stay at your place after all. Thanks very much for inviting me, though."

"Oh, that's all right, dear. Good, I'm glad you've got your dad back. Lots of love to everyone and speak to your soon."

"Yes, thanks. Bye."

"Bye, Jaimini."

I replaced the phone and looked around. All of a sudden the house seemed amazingly silent. I went into the garden to get away from the silence and after a few minutes the phone rang, which made me jump.

What if it was Melanie phoning back ... or, worse still, Luce? I went into the garden and blocked my ears till it had stopped ringing.

Chapter 4

Deciding that food was always a good idea, I went into the kitchen and made some toast. While I was waiting for it, I began to think about Dad. Mum's original idea was not to phone him, so that he wouldn't worry, but now everything was different, wasn't it? Maybe Mum had forgotten all about Dad. That was quite a possibility. After all, she must have been really frightened when everything started speeding up and she had to be rushed to hospital in an ambulance. So what was I supposed to say if Dad phoned?

I was thinking so hard that I let the toast burn and had to put some more under the grill, and it wasn't until the second side was done that I'd made up my mind what to do. When Dad phoned I'd simply say that Mum was asleep, but she was fine.

While I was eating my toast, followed by a huge

bowl of ice cream, I watched television, then finally I switched it off and started on my home-work. It seemed horribly quiet, so I switched the television back on again. Then I got the shock of my life because the phone rang. Right, this was probably Dad. I rehearsed what I was going to say as I went to answer it.

"Hi Jaimini, it's Leah."

"Oh, hi, Leah."

"I was wondering how your mum was, and also I was wondering if you could help with this maths homework I've got."

"Mum's gone into hospital already to have her stitch put in. She'll be back tomorrow, though…"

"Oh, your poor mum! I hope she'll be all right."

"So do I. I can't stop thinking about her all the time."

"Oh, poor you."

Leah was always so sympathetic and kind to everyone. I knew she was dying to get on to the maths homework but she probably thought it was a bit callous to change the subject too quickly. At least she didn't know Dad was away, otherwise I'd have to go into the whole thing about staying the night at Luce's again.

"What was the maths, anyway?"

"Oh, yeah. It's equations…"

So Leah read out her questions and I wrote

them down, then talked her through how she had to do them. Once she'd understood the theory, she said she'd manage the others on her own.

The house seemed even quieter after I put the phone down, and it was getting a bit dark outside. I decided I'd go into every single room and just check there wasn't anybody there. I mean, I *knew* there couldn't possibly be anybody there, but it was worth checking anyway before it got completely dark because I was sure I was going to be really scared when it was time to go to bed. Goodness knows why, because I'd stayed in on my own quite a few times before. So what was so different now?

Turning the television off so that I could listen to every single sound while I was checking each room, I decided that the difference now was the fact that this time I would be spending the whole night on my own. That put a completely different slant on things.

I shut all the upstairs windows and even checked inside all the wardrobes and under the beds. Downstairs it didn't feel half as spooky as upstairs, but all the same I decided to sing to show myself that I wasn't even scared at all. The singing didn't last too long, though, because it stopped me from being able to hear if there were any alien noises around.

With the television on all evening I tried to

immerse myself in my history project. At one point I needed to look up something in a book which was in my bedroom, but I was too much of a coward to go upstairs, so I just missed that bit out.

"What are you going to do when it's bed time, Jaimini," I asked myself, "if you can't actually bring yourself to go upstairs?"

I considered sleeping on the settee but I knew I wouldn't be comfortable, and I didn't want to lie there wide awake, so finally, at ten-fifteen, I decided I'd have to brace myself and face the stairs. It was as I was hovering on the bottom step that I nearly fell off it because the phone rang yet again. Against the silent, still background it sounded as though the volume had been turned right up, and my heart hammered loudly to match it.

For some reason, I didn't want to answer it. It was too late to be one of my friends, and it couldn't be the hospital because Mum would have given them Luce's number. What about Dad? No, it was too late for Dad to ring, too. He always rang between six and seven when he was away. Always. The phone seemed like the enemy at that moment and I put my hands over my ears and started counting the rings. I told myself that it wouldn't go past twenty because nobody went past twenty. I was up to six when it stopped because it had already done a few rings before I started counting.

The relief I felt when it stopped was wonderful, but it only lasted for a few seconds because I could still hear the sound of the phone inside my head and it wouldn't go away.

"Right, pull yourself together," I told myself sternly, but I couldn't stop picturing Luce's lovely, friendly, bustling, noisy house, and half of me wanted to give in and stay there after all. I sat down on the stairs and thought seriously about this idea, then dismissed it. When I thought back to how underhand Luce was being, I could immediately feel my hackles rising.

I kept this emotion firmly in my mind as I got up and slowly faced the rest of the stairs, then went into the bathroom where I cleaned my teeth, went to the loo and washed my face as noisily as I could. Scampering into my bedroom, I drew the curtains, got undressed at a hundred miles an hour, then bolted under the bedclothes.

The book I was reading was a horror story, so I got back out of bed and found *Little Women*, which was easier to cope with, then I got back out of bed again and found the *Giant Joke Book*, which was even better. I must have been relaxed because twice I laughed out loud.

As I laughed aloud for the third time, my laughter froze in my throat because I thought I heard something. No, it wasn't my imagination, it was a noise from downstairs. My whole body went stiff and my heart sounded like someone practising the drums. I held my breath and listened like I've never listened before or since.

About ten seconds later there was another noise, and I realized with horror that I hadn't locked the back door! What a stupid thing to forget to do, and now I was paying for it. A burglar was inside the house, helping himself to our things, and I was lying here, listening to him and unable to move because I was so struck with terror. What would Mum do if we were here on our own and she knew I'd already gone to sleep? I wondered.

When another noise sounded a few seconds later I got up and crept on shaky legs to my chair, lifted it up without a sound and put it under my door handle. I'd seen people do this on television. It didn't really look as though it would stop anyone coming into the room if they wanted to, so I began piling things on to the chair, heavy books and things.

What happened next nearly made me faint on the spot. I heard a scratching on my door! I wasn't mistaken. There was no escaping the horrific fact that there was definitely someone on the other side of my door! I was rooted to the floor and wanted to cry, but I didn't dare make a single sound. Even if my legs *could* have moved I wouldn't have risked going back over to my bed.

I know I've never believed that there is a God before, I gabbled inside my head, *but I promise I'll always believe in you from now on, if you'll just make this burglar go away and never come back...*

A few seconds later, the worst noise of all reached my ears, a sort of vocal ghostly sound. When I heard that, I thought I really was going to collapse, so I sunk to the floor as silently as I could and sat bunched up, hugging my knees and trying to keep my sweating hands from losing their hold on each other.

There followed the worst five minutes of my life, while I sat so tensely I'm surprised I didn't strain every muscle in my body. There was no more scratching, just utter silence, but I couldn't be certain whether the burglar had gone or was still there, not a metre away from me, knowing how scared I was. The final horror came in the form of heavy footsteps coming up the stairs, fast. At that point I let out a long scream and watched in sickening horror as the books tumbled from the chair and my door opened.

"Jaimini? Jaimini, are you all right?"

It was Dad. I burst into tears and jumped up and into his arms, where he held me tight and said, "It's all right now," over and over again.

It took me ages to stop crying, and Dad didn't

press me to talk until I was ready. We went downstairs together, me still doing the occasional involuntary sob as Dad put lights on everywhere. He put the kettle on, then disappeared for about ten seconds, coming back with a big sweater of Mum's.

"You must be freezing. Put that on and tell me what on earth you're doing here all on your own. And why didn't you answer the phone? I phoned you at Lucy's first because that's where Mum said you would be, then I phoned here. When there was no reply I didn't know what on earth to make of it. I just jumped straight into the car and came home."

"But how could you have done, Dad? I thought you were about four hours away."

"I was."

"But the phone only rang about an hour ago."

"Well, that wasn't me. I rang ages ago, and Lucy's mother said you'd just phoned to say that I was back home. So I rang here to find out what was going on, and it got me worried that there was no reply. That's why I decided I'd come straight back."

"It's a long story," I said, feeling embarrassed and stupid all of a sudden.

"Come on, let's hear it."

Now that Dad was certain I was safe and sound, he was beginning to sound a little less sympathetic, and no wonder. I started to tell him my side of the story, and once I'd started I found I couldn't stop.

"I'm really sorry, Dad. It's just that Mum arranged for me to stay at Luce's, but she only told me at the last minute and I didn't want to upset her, so I just agreed to go, but then I phoned Melanie and told her you were home after all, so that I wouldn't have to go. You see, Luce and I aren't friends. She's being really horrible to me and I couldn't bear to stay with her, so I decided it would be best if I just stayed here. But I didn't know it would be this scary. I heard noises, you see. It wasn't you, it was before you got here... An awful scratching and a weird sort of ghostly, wailing noise. I didn't imagine it, Dad, honestly. There really *was* someone outside my bedroom door..."

"Hold on a sec. Calm down. I'm sure you're right about there being someone. And that someone was Lucy."

"What!"

"As I drew up in the car, I saw someone running off. I'm sure it was Lucy..."

"Well, what did she look like?"

"She looked like Lucy, of course. *Just* like her. I'm certain I wasn't mistaken. I thought that maybe you'd changed your plans and decided to have Lucy to stay over here with you. I have to admit I couldn't work out why she was running around outside, but knowing you two and the things you get up to, I figured anything was possible."

I hadn't really been listening to a single word Dad had said after, "*I'm sure it was Lucy...*" My mind was fully occupied with trying to imagine if Luce could really be so horrible she'd try and scare me to death like that. It seemed impossible that it could have been her. Dad must have been mistaken. After all, it was dark. He couldn't have seen properly. I tried to put myself in Luce's place. I imagined myself being utterly offended and upset because my best friend, who I didn't really like at the time, had refused to stay the night with me. I imagined Luce realizing that I'd made it up about Dad coming home because I couldn't bear to stay the night with her. But, even taking all that into consideration, I still couldn't see Luce deliberately coming round here to pay me back like that...

On the other hand, Luce *was* the crazy one. I knew her mind didn't work like other people's. Maybe she was having a weird sort of brainstorm? It wouldn't be the first time that that had happened. I suddenly realized I'd been miles away and Dad had said something about Mum.

"So Mum phoned you and explained everything, did she?" I asked him.

He nodded and smiled. "She's in the best place

she can be at the moment," he said. "Once she's got this stitch in, everything should be OK."

I didn't say anything, just wished that Mum was back home with us and telling us that everything was fine again. We drank our tea, then Dad sent me up to bed and assured me that he would lock the back door, and there was nothing to worry about any more. We even went all round the house together to check that everything was as it should be and nothing was missing.

"Aren't you cross with me?" I asked impulsively, as I went out of the kitchen to go to bed. Goodness knows why I asked that. I think it may have been the instinctive feeling that if we didn't get it out of the way tonight, it might be brought up the following day with much worse consequences.

"It's late and I'm tired, so I don't want to go into what it is that's gone wrong between you and Luce, but I can't say that I'm happy about the way you've acted. Melanie Edmunson sounded very puzzled when I asked to speak to you."

"What did you say to her?" I asked, feeling worried again.

"I smoothed it over by saying I was on my way home and that I just guessed that you might be there as there was no reply at home. Then I quickly added that you must have been out in the garden or something."

"Thanks, Dad."

"See you in the morning."

"Yeah, night."

The following morning seemed to arrive very quickly, and I leapt out of bed, feeling happy that Mum would soon be back. When I thought about school, my spirits took a bit of a dive because I was dreading having to see Luce.

I had to *make* myself go into our registration room, and the relief when I realized she wasn't there was enormous. I started talking to Alex Drew because she was the only person not talking to anyone else, and I wanted to be occupied when Luce came in. After a couple of minutes Leoni Weston came in, and Alex immediately jumped up and went over to chat to her best friend, practically cutting me off mid-sentence. I could see them talking behind their hands and glancing over very obviously in my direction, and I made a resolution never to try to be friendly with either of those two girls again because it was obvious they didn't like me.

Luce never did turn up, which in itself seemed very suspicious. I told Tash discreetly about what had happened the previous night, though I didn't mention anything about intruders. I just said Dad had turned up out of the blue.

During lessons I sat with Evi Bligh most of the

time. She was really being nice to me, and it made me wonder why I'd never been particularly friendly with her before. I was still curious about why she hadn't wanted me to report that boy, but I didn't bring it up because I thought it might be hurtful. She asked me if I was going down to the café after school and I said I was, and she said she was too, because Tash had asked her.

So after school, Tash and Evi went down to the café. Leah was on duty. Fen and Andy had a sports practice and I went home to see Mum, but we all decided to meet up at the café afterwards.

I ran the whole way home and saw that Dad's car was still there.

"Hi, it's me!"

Taking the stairs two at a time, I found Mum in bed and Dad sitting in a chair beside her.

"Have you got the stitch in? Are you OK now?" I gabbled, as I kissed Mum.

"Yes and yes," Mum replied happily. "Only I've got to stay in bed a lot and take things easy for a while."

"But otherwise, everything's going to be OK?"

Mum nodded happily, then told me all about the hospital and the nurses and some of the patients she'd met. I kept wondering when she was going to mention the previous night, but she never did and I realized that Dad must have decided not to tell her. He probably didn't want to upset her. Good, that was one weight off my mind.

"Is it OK if I go to the café to meet the others?" I asked, after a bit.

"Don't be long," was all Mum said, and Dad smiled rather absentmindedly, so I beat a hasty retreat, and thought that although Mum was going through a horrible time, the one good thing about it all was that I was getting off terribly lightly because nothing else was important in our house, except Mum's health!

When I went into the café, the first sight that met my eyes was that of two boys at a table with Alex Drew and Leoni Weston. For some reason or other I felt instinctively angry when I saw them, yet I couldn't put my finger on why. Frowning, I walked over to join Andy, Fen, Tash and Evi.

"How's your mum?" Fen asked straightaway, and the others seemed really interested. I told them briefly, but it was as though they were waiting for me to say more, so I began to tell them a few things that Mum had said about the other patients. As I talked I realized they were hanging on to my every word and I really couldn't work out why they were so interested in hospitals all of a sudden.

It wasn't until I'd finished and everyone was quiet, that I sussed what the problem was. Something must have happened before I arrived, some sort of argument, because none of the other four seemed to feel like talking, not even Tash. They'd only been interested in my chatter because I'd broken the silence. I raised my eyebrows to Tash as subtly as I could, but she looked the other way, which made me wonder if the problem was something to do with me. Maybe everybody knew about how I'd deliberately not stayed at Luce's, and they were all cross with me for being horrible.

I was just wondering whether to make up some excuse to go, so that I could get away from this horrible atmosphere, when I glanced over at those two boys and met the eyes of one of them again. Bingo! I knew now why I'd felt so inexplicably angry. It was because the boy I was looking at was the one who had attacked Evi. I was sure of it.

"Evi, it was *him*, wasn't it!" I whispered loudly and somewhat triumphantly, tipping my head to indicate who I meant.

"What?" she asked, and the others all turned round to see who I was talking about.

"The boy who attacked you... That's him sitting over there, isn't it?"

"No ... no, it wasn't him. I don't even know him."

"But..."

"But someone did attack you, Evi, didn't

they?" asked Tash, full of concern.

"It wasn't anything much…"

I was just about to protest, when I remembered how closed up Evi had been on the subject the last time I'd confronted her. But I was so certain that I was right about the boys that I couldn't leave it alone.

"I know you don't want to talk about it, but just tell me if it *was* him, then I won't say another word on the subject, I promise."

"It wasn't him, no," she replied, firmly.

"Why did he attack you?" asked Fen.

"Nobody attacked me and I don't want to talk about it, OK?" she replied, turning to look squarely at me. There was a definite gleam in her eye, which I'd never seen before.

"Let's leave it, Jaimini, shall we?" said Tash, and looking round the table I realized they were all giving me warning looks. I couldn't understand why everyone was being so protective towards Evi all of a sudden, and yet no one except me was interested in getting to the heart of the one thing they *could* help her with.

A few minutes later we all decided to go home. The conversation had been so stilted, it was quite a relief to split up. Fen and Andy went off first, but Tash wanted to see Leah about some homework that they both had to do, so she went off to the kitchen to find her. Evi said she was going to the loo, so I suddenly decided to have a quick word with those boys. I was eaten up with curiosity. It didn't matter if Evi saw me at their table, because I could easily have been talking to Alex and Leoni. I was very nervous about talking to them because I didn't want to find myself being pushed around the following day, so I'd decided to go in gently.

"Sorry to butt in, but can I ask you something?" I said to the boy who had met my eyes earlier on.

All four of them looked up at me as though I was their mother telling them to go to bed or something.

I decided to go ahead and ask, even though nobody had actually said anything.

"Do you know who could have picked on Evi Bligh the other day, because for some reason or other she doesn't want to tell anyone...?"

"I'm not surprised she doesn't want—" said the other boy, the one I didn't really recognize. He never finished the sentence, though, because the first boy interrupted him.

"Shut up, Pete."

His eyes were fixed on something just behind me. I turned round and there stood Evi. I couldn't read the expression on her face, but I didn't like it.

"What were you saying?" I asked the boy who

had been interrupted, even though I was feeling more nervous than ever. In fact, I was shaking because by now Alex and Leoni were scowling at me, and the atmosphere was awful.

"Nothing," he mumbled, looking at his empty glass.

"Time I was going," said Alex, standing up. "Coming, George?"

"Yeah, I reckon," he answered, and they all got up and shuffled over to the counter to pay.

Tash was just emerging from the kitchen and Evi turned without a word to me and went over to her. I waited for them for a moment, but they were both talking to Jan, so I just went on my own, with my whirling thoughts.

Why was everything so mysterious and puzzling all of a sudden? There were so many questions in my mind, and no answers at all. If only I could talk it all through with someone. Luce, for instance. But Luce was the one person I definitely couldn't talk to.

Or could I?

Once I'd had the thought, it wouldn't leave me alone, and there and then I made a decision. The very next day I would have this whole thing out with Luce, and if she wasn't at school I'd go to her house after school. I couldn't carry on like this. I needed my best friend back, because I missed her.

Chapter 5

Although I was dreading having to have a big talk with Luce, I was still determined to do it. I really wanted to talk to her somewhere on our own, but there wasn't anywhere at school where we could guarantee not being interrupted. In the end I thought that perhaps it would be better to wait till after school and go to the café. We could tell the others that we wanted to talk on our own for a little while. They would understand.

I was all ready to deliver this speech to Luce the moment that I walked into the registration room, but she wasn't there.

Not again! I thought, but then I caught sight of her school bag on her desk, so I looked all around, but Luce herself was nowhere to be seen. I decided she must have just gone to the loo or something. Evi was standing by the open door, watching me.

"Have you seen Luce?" I asked her.

"No, sorry," she replied, then off she went, presumably to her own registration room.

I thought of asking Leoni and Alex, who were chatting away in the corner, but decided not to. Then it suddenly occurred to me that perhaps this wasn't Luce's bag at all. Maybe someone else had an identical one? It was quite a common design. I opened up the top, pulled out a couple of books and saw instantly that it *was* Luce's.

By the time we went into assembly and she still hadn't appeared I began to feel really puzzled. I was frustrated because now I wouldn't be able to see her till morning break as we were in different work groups.

The moment the bell went I flew back to our registration room, only to find it completely empty. I felt so disappointed, and was about to go off to join the others when who should walk in but Luce.

"Hi," I said tentatively, noticing the slightly embarrassed, slightly hacked-off look on her face.

"Hi," she replied, in a rather unfriendly voice.

"Are you better?" I asked.

She just nodded.

"What was the matter?"

"Sick."

"Oh."

I'd had some awkward conversations in my time, but this one really took the biscuit.

"Luce, can we try and sort a few things out?"

"What, like how come you lied to Mum yesterday?"

I blushed when she said that. I'm lucky, though: when I blush it doesn't show to anyone else, I just feel very hot.

"Look, I'm really sorry, but how could I stay the night with you when you're obviously not friends with me?"

"*I'm* not friends with *you*! That's rich!"

"What do you mean?"

"I mean that it's the other way round. *You're* not friends with *me*."

"Why? What have I done?"

"You know very well what you've done!"

"I don't know what on earth you're on about. All I know is that you're trying to stop me entering the story competition, presumably so that you can have the way clear for your own entry!"

"What rot! I'm not even entering a story!"

We were raising our voices, but we didn't care.

"Then why did your mum go and get the last copy of *Our Times*?"

"Maybe she just wanted to buy it for herself. And while we're on the subject of competitions, what gives you the right to tell Kevin that you don't think I ought to be allowed to enter the cookery competition because my mum's a caterer?"

"I didn't tell Kevin that!"

"Kevin says you did."

"Well, Kevin's wrong, because I didn't."

"Well…"

She didn't know what to say to that. Personally, I couldn't believe what I was hearing. I'd never go and say a thing like that to Kevin. I couldn't care less *who* entered the cookery competition.

"Well, anyway, why did you steal my tenner?"

"What!"

Now, this I couldn't believe. I stared at Luce as though she had just told me she was going to take off for the moon in twenty seconds.

"It's no good trying to look all innocent. You were seen rootling about in my bag."

"Who by?"

"Alex and Leoni, if you must know."

I knew those two girls had it in for me. They made me sick.

"It's true I looked in your bag, but only to see if it *was* your bag, because *you* were nowhere to be seen."

"I was getting the science off Fen."

"Look, Luce, I didn't take your tenner, honestly. What do you think I am? A monster? I'd never dream of taking your money."

"Well, someone's taken it…" She was sounding less stroppy, thank goodness, but I was feeling awful. This conversation was supposed to clear

77

things up between us, and all it was doing was making things even worse. Suddenly I'd had enough. I sat down with my arms on my desk, put my head on my arms and tried not to cry.

"Oh Jaimini, don't cry," Luce instantly said, but she didn't put her arm round me or anything.

"I'm just so depressed about everything. I swear I never spoke to Kevin, and I double swear I never took your tenner."

"And I swear I'm not entering the story competition."

I raised my head slowly from my desk and looked at Luce. Neither of us knew what to say so we stayed completely silent, and it was at that point that one of the teachers, Mr Hawkenbury – or old Hawkeye, as we all call him – flung open the door and said, "Come on, everybody out. It's a lovely day. We don't want to be sitting around here with glum indoor faces now, do we?"

He had spoken to us as though we were about four and a half, beamed brightly, then rushed off again, singing as he went. I don't know what it was that suddenly seemed so hysterically funny, but Luce and I cracked up and couldn't stop for ages.

"Come on, let's call a truce," I said, as we got up to take Old Hawkeye's advice and go outside for the last bit of break.

"It's all been a big misunderstanding, obviously," Luce commented in the corridor. "And knowing me, it's probably my fault, as usual."

"No, it's not your fault. I shouldn't have jumped to conclusions so quickly about the story competition."

I frowned and wondered why on earth Kevin had said what he'd said. I was going to find out the moment school was over. I also wondered what had happened to Luce's tenner, though I had a pretty good idea who had nicked it and pinned the blame on me. Those two girls had a lot to answer for. I began to wonder whether or not they were in with those two boys, Pete and George. Maybe all four of them were victimizing poor Evi? If only Evi would trust us enough to tell us what the problem was, then we could do something to help her.

On our way down to the netball courts (where we knew the others would be), we passed Alex and Leoni.

"Look, it's them. I'm going to confront them," Luce said, a determined look appearing on her face.

"No, just ignore them," I said, because I suddenly didn't feel I could face any more confrontations. I just wanted to forget everything. I could put up with Alex and Leoni being horrible now I'd got Luce back. Then the moment I'd had that nice contented thought, I stopped abruptly and went rigid with horror.

"Whatever's the matter?" Luce asked.

The matter was that I'd suddenly remembered the biggest reason of all I had for not being friends with Luce. How I could have forgotten this? My mind went straight back to two nights before and in an instant I was curled up on my bedroom floor again, filled with terror. Then I was in Dad's arms, crying with relief, and I could hear his voice just as clearly as if he was talking to me then and there. "*As I drew up in the car, I saw someone running off. I'm sure it was Lucy...*"

"Did you..." I began, then found that I couldn't carry on. Dad must have been wrong.

"Did I what?"

I realized in that moment that I didn't actually *have* to know the answer, did I? I mean, Luce and I were friends again. If she'd done something totally insanely silly, she wouldn't want to have it dredged up and talked about now, would she? She'd apologize soon enough. I'd just have to wait a little longer until she felt sure that I hadn't been the one to speak to Kevin after all, and that I also hadn't been responsible for taking her ten-pound note. Then she would talk to me like she used to, and maybe we'd even manage to laugh about that scary night one day. But now was not the time to be discussing it.

"Jaimini? Did I what?"

"Did you know that Mum will have to stay in

bed till the end of her pregnancy, more or less?"

"No, I didn't. That's terrible. Your poor mum! Does she know if it's going to be a boy or a girl yet?"

"Well, if she does, she hasn't told me."

"Aren't you dying to know?"

"No, I'd rather have a surprise."

"Yes, I suppose that would be much more exciting."

And so we carried on chatting on our own, and then with the others till the end of break. It was nice to be back to normal again. Well, more or less back to normal. There were still one or two mysteries to clear up.

It was during PSE that our wonderful new-found friendship hit the rocks. PSE is the one subject, apart from games and PE, that all six of us do together.

"Now, I'm setting two different tasks for homework this week," Mrs Merle said. "Those of you who *haven't* entered the literary competition, I'd like you to have a shot at writing a short story on an environmental theme; I'd like the rest of you to get into pairs and do a short project on the same theme. It's a very broad subject so you've got plenty of scope. You've also got plenty of time, because I'm giving you three weeks as I know how busy you are with your other subjects. I thought it would be a nice idea to have our own separate class competition. I'll look at all your projects and stories, then award two prizes – one for the best project and one for the best story."

Mrs Merle is always so fair about everything I could tell that the rest of the class thought it was a really good idea to have the two competitions. Personally I was getting fed up with the very word "competition" because there seemed to be so many of them about at the moment – this one, the cookery one and the literary one. The only one I was interested in was the literary one.

I was just wondering who to do my project with because Luce would be doing the story as she didn't enter the competition, when Mrs Merle asked for a show of hands of those who would be doing the short story. Luce's hand went up, naturally. Mrs Merle wrote down each person's name but when she got to Luce she said, "Lucy, you entered the competition, didn't you?"

"No, I didn't," said Luce, going red.

"I saw your entry, Luce. Come on, you may be keen to write another story, but I'm afraid it's a project from you, please."

Mrs Merle smiled and carried on writing down names, not realizing the turmoil she had just created inside my head. I looked at Fen and Tash and saw a worried look pass between them. Leah and Andy were whispering to each other and didn't seem to be aware of anything going on between the rest of us. Luce herself was bright pink, and I could feel my temper mounting.

There was no need for me to say anything. I'd been right all along. That was it. If Luce thought she could lie to me and go on being my best friend, she had another think coming. I scowled and turned away from her.

"I'll do the project with you if you want," said Evi.

Just then Mrs Merle spoke.

"Evi, I didn't know you'd entered the literary competition?"

"Yes, I handed my entry in to Mrs Crowhurst."

"Oh right, that's fine."

So I said I'd do the project with Evi, because I really didn't care who I did the project with. All I could think about was that Luce had lied to me about this most important thing. And that's how we got back to square one again. I could see Tash was in a state because she knew Luce and I had fallen out, but I couldn't help that, could I? She – Tash – was trying to talk Luce into doing something or saying something, but Luce just kept shaking her head and looking stubborn.

I pointedly didn't speak to Luce for the rest of the day, and she didn't speak to me either. Luce went straight home after school, and the rest of us went down separately to the café. I was only going because I wanted to talk to Kevin. Tash was on duty, and she walked down with Evi, while Fen set off with Andy and Leah.

Sitting down with the others I sensed straight away that Fen was stressed about something. It didn't take me long to work out what it was. She waited till Evi went to choose a cake at the counter, then whispered to me.

"Guess who's helping Tash with her story?"

"Who?"

"Evi."

"Don't you like her?"

"There's something about her that I'm not a hundred per cent sure about. She's suddenly latched on to us lot, and we don't know what to say when she's around."

"Is that why you all hung on my every word in the café yesterday?" I asked.

Fen smiled. "You noticed, then?"

"But Tash seems to be fond of her."

"Who are you talking about?" Andy asked, her big eyes glowing with intrigue. Beside her, Leah's face looked very pale.

"Evi," whispered Fen.

"I feel sorry for her," said Leah. "She's never really had any friends. And she likes us lot."

"That's true, and she's never done anything to us, has she?" Andy added, supporting Leah.

"'Spose not," I agreed, but Fen just wrinkled up her nose.

"Jaimini, don't be too hard on Luce," Leah suddenly said.

"I think it's better if we don't discuss Luce," I said. I must have said it rather abruptly, because the others all looked taken aback.

"There's a lot of stuff that you don't know about, you see," I added.

"We're all staying friends with both of you until you get things sorted out," said Andy firmly. She looked round at the others. "Right?"

"Right," said Fen and Leah.

"Well, I'm just going to have a quick word with Kevin," I said. "And ... thanks for being so..." I didn't know what to say that didn't sound too formal or gooey. I just wanted to thank them for being so sensible and nice.

"For being so utterly, wonderfully, magnanimously, heroically brilliant? Is that what you're trying to say, Jaimes?" asked Andy, with a deadpan face.

"Yeah, something like that," I agreed with a grin, as I went off to the kitchen.

"Kevin?"

"That's my name. You don't have to whisper it, it doesn't suffer from wear and tear, you know," he answered, in typical Kevin style.

"Did you tell Luce that I said she shouldn't enter the cookery competition because of her mum being a caterer, and people thinking that

85

Luce might have cheated?"

"Well, those weren't my exact words, but I gather you were quite concerned that people might think that, and I thought it was quite a reasonable concern, to be honest. In fact, I really should have thought of it myself. That's why I decided to make it the rule that none of you lot is allowed to enter. I didn't want to be too mean on Luce, so I included you all. It wouldn't look very good if one of you won, when you work here, would it? People would automatically assume it was fixed."

I think that was probably the longest speech I'd ever heard Kevin make in all the time I'd known him.

"But who told you what I'd said?"

"Er? Who was it now?" he said thoughtfully, as he sifted icing sugar over a gateau. "I think it was … yes, it was Andy."

"Andy!"

I went back into the café just as Andy was going out of the door. I rushed over and breathlessly asked her if she had told Kevin that I said that Luce shouldn't enter the cookery competition because of her mum being a caterer.

"Yeah, I did," she said. "You were quite right to be worried about what people would think, Jaimini."

"But who told you that I'd said that?"

"Um … Leah, I think. Yes, I'm pretty sure it was Leah. I've got to go. I'm supposed to be looking after Sebastien. I'd completely forgotten." (Sebastien is Andy's one-year-old brother, by the way.)

This was getting silly! I rushed back to Leah, who was on her way to phone her sister.

"Leah, did you tell Andy that I said that Luce shouldn't enter that cookery competition because of her mum being a caterer?"

Leah looked really worried. "Well, you *did* say that, didn't you?" she asked me.

"Who told *you* I said that?" I asked, ignoring her question.

"Er … Fen, I think. Yes, it was Fen."

Now this really *was* ridiculous! I went over to Fen, who was sitting in silence with Evi. Just as I was on the point of asking her the same question, Tash came rushing in from the kitchen looking really worried.

"Your mum's just phoned. She wants you to get back home straight away."

"Omigod! I'd forgotten I was supposed to go straight home today! Oh, I'm so stupid! Oh, poor mum! Has anything happened? Tell me that nothing's happened!"

"I don't know. She just said to be as quick as you can. She didn't sound too good, Jaimes. Hurry."

I've never run so hard in all my life. Not ever. I felt so guilty and so worried. I wanted to punish myself for being such a thoughtless daughter. You see, during the day, we'd arranged it so that Mum always had someone to look after her or at least had a neighbour at the other end of the phone who could rush over if necessary. It's important for Mum to stay in bed as much as possible so the stitch doesn't come out. Apart from going to the loo, she's not really supposed to get out of bed for anything. She can move about the bedroom very slowly, but that's all.

Mrs Danin had to go out at four o'clock so we had arranged for me to come straight home, but being so wrapped up in my own problems I'd completely forgotten. There must be something urgently wrong for Mum to have phoned the café and told me to come home, and I couldn't bear to think that it was my fault. As I hurled myself through the back door I started praying like mad.

I dashed through the kitchen into the hall, where Mum was sitting on the bottom stair looking pale and drawn.

"Oh Mum, I'm really sorry. Are you OK? What are you doing out of bed?"

"The doctor's on her way," she said, in scarcely more than a whisper.

"What's happened?" I asked, feeling my heart racing with fear.

"I let the receiver drop off the bedside cabinet and it dragged the rest of the phone down with it and that pulled the lead out of the socket.

"Oh Mum, you didn't try to move the wardrobe to fix it back in, did you?"

"Well, I had to have the phone, didn't I?"

I could feel the tears gathering behind my eyes and my throat was hurting.

"When I couldn't manage it, I thought I'd better come down here to phone you, but I'm sure the stitch has come out. I've phoned the doctor and now I daren't move."

"I'll help you up to bed, Mum."

My voice was soft and choked, the lump in my throat was so big.

Chapter 6

I hardly slept a wink that night. The doctor said the stitch was still in place and no damage had been done, but she was wrong. I had damaged Mum's confidence in me. She couldn't rely on me any more. I'd apologized and apologized, and Mum had kept on assuring me it was all right. She wasn't holding it against me, but the problem was *I* was holding it against myself. I said I'd give up the café for the next two weeks to make up for it, but Mum told me not to be silly. She was being so kind to me, it made me feel even worse. She didn't even tell Dad anything about the telephone episode.

The next day at school was a strange one, partly because I was walking about in a daze, I was so tired. Evi had been to see Mrs Merle to ask if Tash could do a project with her, instead of a story, and Mrs Merle had agreed. I was quite relieved to be doing my project on my own, but I began to understand why Fen didn't trust Evi Bligh. Luce and I weren't speaking to each other. Fen was totally fed up with Tash for spending all her time with Evi. Only Andy and Leah seemed unaffected by everything.

I had decided to throw myself into my project because I simply had to get my mind off all the other bad things in my life. So, although I had thought that it was going to be quite a boring thing to do, it turned out to be very interesting and absorbing. I was doing the project on re-cycling and I'd got lots of ideas for it. I stayed in at the morning break and lunch time working on the project and managed to get up to page seven by the beginning of afternoon school.

That afternoon I had games and then I was going to go straight home, but when I phoned Mum at lunch time to check that she was all right, she said I was welcome to go to the café. A good friend of hers called Carolyn had dropped in and was staying till six-thirty, apparently. Fen had had a word with me during games; only a brief word, partly because we were both running round the track at the time, and partly because Fen really should have been doing long jump, but she'd sneaked away to talk to me.

"I'm worried about Tash," she began.

I waited for her to go on.

"She's so involved with Evi and I'm not sure that she really wants to be, but you know Tash, she doesn't like trouble."

"Have you talked to Tash about it?"

"I never get the chance, because she's absolutely *always* with Evi. Even today after school they're going to work on their project together at Tash's house."

"Try and persuade Tash to come to the café without Evi and we'll talk to her together, if you want."

"Yeah, OK. I'll try."

"Why not go and see her now while Evi's doing high jump?"

"OK."

"Who's working at the café today?"

"Andy."

"Uh-oh! You'd better go. Miss Tennett's on the war path. Good luck!"

"See you."

At the end of school I walked down to the café with Leah, Andy and Fen. Once again Luce went straight off home, and I must admit I couldn't help feeling sorry for her even though I was still so cross about her lying about the story competition.

"Did you manage to talk to Tash?" I asked Fen.

"Talk to Tash about what?" Leah asked straightaway, then she went pink and said, "Oh sorry, I'm just being nosey. Forget it."

"No, don't forget it. I want to know!" Andy put in, jokingly.

"Fen's worried that Tash is getting sort of led astray by Evi, against her better judgement," I explained, as best I could.

"And now I'm even more worried," said Fen. "You see, I *did* manage to talk to Tash while Evi wasn't around, but it was only for a minute or two near the beginning of games, and Tash admitted that she *was* finding it quite heavy-going, but said she didn't know how to get out of the friendship now. She said she felt really sorry for Evi, but all the same she found it quite claustrophobic being friends with her."

"What did she mean by that?" Leah asked.

"I think she meant that Evi never seemed to let her out of her sight. Apparently she was even trying to persuade Tash to let her join the Café Club, then when Tash explained that there were only six days in the week, so that we only needed six people, Evi started trying to get Tash to agree to drop one of the existing members."

"Which one of us did she want to drop?" Andy asked.

"Either me or Jaimes," replied Fen.

"Hm," said Andy with a thoughtful look I recognized on her face. It was a look that said *I can read more into this situation than you can, and*

I don't like what I'm reading.

"What's that 'Hm' mean?" asked Leah.

"It means, isn't it interesting that she wants to get rid of the two people who are the biggest threats to her?"

"Me? A threat? Why?" I asked, feeling totally baffled.

"Because you're the brainy one. You work things out."

"And why me? *I'm* not the brainy one," Fen pointed out.

"You're a threat because you're Tash's best friend. And Evi wants Tash for her own best friend."

"I reckon Evi's got it wrong, because I might be labelled the brainy one, but it looks as though it's *you* who's got it all worked out!" I smiled at Andy.

"I may be completely wrong. I've just never been too sure about Evi Bligh," Andy said, staring at something in the distance.

"Me neither," we all slowly agreed.

"The thing that really has got me worried," went on Fen, "is that Tash admitted to me that she'd actually planned to try and gently drop Evi and her friendship the moment their project was completed."

"Why did that get you worried? I would have thought you'd be relieved," said Leah.

"No, the thing that got me worried was that

when I'd just finished talking to Tash, and she'd gone off to the long jump, and I was about to go to sprinting practice, I noticed Evi standing quite still a few metres away. I gave her something resembling a smile and her expression made my blood run cold."

"What do you mean? What did she look like?" I asked with a tremor in my voice.

"She looked … hard. Yeah … hard."

"Evi? Evi Bligh? Hard?" Leah said, as though she couldn't believe what she was hearing.

"Yeah. That's the only word for it, I'm afraid. And that's why I'm a bit worried."

"Do you think she heard what Tash said?"

"Yes, I've got the horrible feeling she did."

We were silent and thoughtful for the next few minutes till we got to the café, where Andy went in through the back, and Fen, Leah and I went in through the main door.

After we'd ordered drinks and toasted teacakes from Jan, who seemed in a very good mood, Leah wanted me to help her with another load of maths homework. This time it needed a calculator. I was just reaching down to the bottom of my bag to get one, when my eye fell on something that really shook me.

"My project! Omigod! What's on earth's happened to it?"

I pulled out the seven sheets that I'd been so

proud of, only to find that every page was speckled with blobs of Tipp-Ex. The whole project looked like a snow storm had hit it. I couldn't believe it. I just stared at it and tried to work out how on earth it had got into that state.

"However has that happened?" asked Leah, wide-eyed with disbelief.

"Someone doesn't want you to win this competition," Fen said, looking grim.

Of course my mind went straight to Luce. *Not again! I don't believe it.*

"Andy, look," said Leah, tugging on Andy's sleeve as she went past to wipe one of the tables.

"Who's done that?" Andy said, looking as incredulous as the rest of us.

"I don't know," I said, through gritted teeth. This whole competition thing really was getting a bit much.

"I'll be back in a minute; I've just got to serve that lot over there."

And with that Andy went off to table four. I hadn't noticed until then but at table four sat Leoni, Alex, George and Pete.

They seemed deep in conversation and I was glad. I didn't feel comfortable when they were around, because I was convinced they didn't like me.

As it happened Andy didn't return to our table for a bit because she had to rush off to the kitchen for more orders as it was getting fairly crowded in the café.

The rest of us examined my project closely as though the person who'd done this to me might have thoughtfully signed their name somewhere so I could pin the crime on them and get them into deep trouble. None of the others had any bright ideas about who could have done it, and I just felt so depressed because all my hard work was down the drain, and whoever was responsible had managed to get away with it.

"It must have happened during games," I said, as I slowly put it away.

Then Fen suddenly said, "There's something different about this place today, but I can't put my finger on what it is."

At that very moment Andy walked past our table, and just as if she'd heard Fen's comment, she said, "Mark's ill. He's got that virus that's going round."

"That's what it is! Jan and Andy are working flat out because there's no one else here working!"

"What virus?" asked Fen.

"It's awful. My sister's had it. There aren't really any symptoms except you haven't got any energy and you have a really high temperature," said Leah.

"Isn't that what Luce had?" Fen asked me.

I felt embarrassed that I didn't really know.

"I thought ... she felt sick," I stammered.

"Yes, but mainly she had a really high temperature. I know, because Mum met Luce's mum yesterday and Melanie was telling Mum that Luce had such a high temperature that day she had to go home from school, that Melanie and Terry took turns to sit with her until three o'clock in the morning because they were scared in case it turned out to be something like meningitis."

I could feel my throat contracting as Fen was speaking. One of the things which had been puzzling me had now been answered.

"You mean Tuesday night?" I asked in a small voice.

"That's right. Tuesday," said Fen, wrinkling her eyebrows.

I leaned back in my chair and felt suddenly rather weak. I think I was weak with relief that now I knew it couldn't have been Luce who had deliberately tried to scare me witless on Tuesday night. I don't think I could have stayed friends with someone who had done that to me, and that's why I'd avoided asking Luce about it. Subconsciously, I didn't want to know if it *had* been her.

The relief of knowing that it wasn't Luce after all was so great that I'd forgotten until then to consider who had been inside my house that night. The others were all chatting away, but I sat silently with my thoughts, then after a little while I began to think I must have imagined the whole thing.

"Look what's turned up!" Andy said, eyes bright, thrusting a ten-pound note in front of us all.

"Ten pounds. Big deal," said Leah, but then Fen took it carefully from Andy's fingers and breathed out slowly.

"Not just any old ten-pound note. *The* ten-pound note. Where did you get it, Andy?"

"What do you mean, *the* ten-pound note?" asked Leah. I had been wondering that, too.

Fen spread it out on the table, and we all saw a red splodge on the note.

"It's Luce's," breathed Leah.

"Hang on a sec," I said. "How do you all know that this is Luce's?"

"Because we saw Luce's ten-pound note before it got stolen, and this is definitely the same one. I mean, it's not every day you come across a ten-pound note with a red splodge like that on it, is it?"

"Where did you get it, Andy?"

"Table four," Andy replied. "George."

"George? So *he* nicked Luce's tenner. Luce thinks it was *me*!" I squeaked. "I'll get that George! What a scumbag!"

"Not so fast, Jaimes," cautioned Andy, but there was no stopping me. I was really mad.

"This is Luce's tenner that you nicked, isn't it?" I said, to a very startled-looking George, without wasting time on preliminaries.

"No, I did *not*," he answered indignantly.

"Well, unfortunately for you, it's a very recognizable note, so I'm afraid you're sussed, George."

George, Pete, Alex and Leoni were all looking at each other. They were having a conversation with their eyes. Not a word was spoken, but I could tell that a great deal of communicating was going on all the same. I tried to follow what they were signalling to each other, but I couldn't, so I just waited.

"What's it to you, anyway?" Pete said, eventually.

"I'll tell you what it is to me. *I'm* the one who's been accused of taking it. I'm supposed to be Luce's best friend and she's convinced I took it, because you two told her that I was rummaging around in her bag," I flung at Alex and Leoni because I was past caring by then, I was so angry.

"We never said that, honestly." Alex defended herself in a surprisingly soft voice. I was expecting her to be much more aggressive, and it disarmed me for a moment.

"Well, what *did* you say then?" I asked, easing up a little.

"We just said that you were the only person we'd seen looking in her bag. We thought she'd gather that we meant that it obviously couldn't have been you, and that we hadn't see anyone else."

"Oh well, Luce got the impression from somewhere or other that it *was* me."

"Probably from Claws," Alex said under her breath to Leoni.

"Claws? Who's Claws?" I asked, thinking at the back of my mind that this was turning into a really silly conversation because we were getting away from the fact that George had nicked Luce's tenner in the first place.

"It doesn't matter," said Pete quickly.

"It does matter to me," I pointed out. "I'm trying to sort things out with Luce, and I want to know if someone is deliberately giving her false information about me."

There followed another of those eye conversations between the four of them while I waited a little less patiently this time.

"Look, can't you just tell me who Claws is?" I interrupted their silent communication.

"Somebody took the tenner from Lucy and gave it to George, because they owed it to him," said Leoni eventually.

My eyes went from one to the other of them, but when they met Alex's eyes, she looked down and I knew then there was more to all this than they were telling me.

I drew up a chair beside Alex, and decided to tackle her on her own.

"Look, I know you don't particularly like me," I began.

"Yes, I do," she answered with great indignation. She looked and sounded so hurt that it completely threw me and I really didn't know what to say next. There was nothing for it but to simply try again.

"Please tell me, who *is* Claws?" I asked, looking at Alex with pleading eyes, and feeling a little surge of happiness that perhaps I'd been wrong after all about Alex and Leoni.

"It's Evi Bligh," Pete said in a flat voice.

"What!" I squeaked. "Poor little Evi who everybody feels so sorry for because she's got no friends?"

"Huh! You're right about one thing. She's certainly got no friends. No one in their right mind would dream of being friends with her. With her as a friend you sure wouldn't need any enemies," George commented fiercely.

"So Evi stole Luce's tenner," I said slowly and thoughtfully.

"Yeah, because she needed to pay George to shut up," Leoni filled me in.

At this point George looked very embarrassed.

"I didn't *ask* for the tenner or anything. She just gave it to me, and said, 'Don't you dare tell that Jaimini Riva why you pushed me, or you're dead.'"

"So it *was* you. I knew I was right," I said triumphantly, but then my brief feeling of triumph disappeared because things were piling up in my mind and there was a thought – a serious thought – trying to get through and grab my attention, but I couldn't grasp what it was.

"But why?" I asked next. "Why ever did you hurt her like that?"

"'Cos of what she did to us," mumbled Pete.

I hardly dared ask, I just waited and George began to speak in a low voice. I thought he was going to start crying at one point, but he managed to keep himself together, with the help of Leoni, who kept her hand on his arm the whole time. I wondered if they were going out with each other, but as George began to talk I realized they weren't.

"She just gets her claws into whoever she wants to be her friend," he began, looking down. "That's why we call her 'Claws'. Anyway, she wanted to be friends with Leoni. She managed to split up Alex and Leoni but she wasn't bargaining on me. She didn't realize that Leoni and I have known each other for years, and I could see what was happening. I knew Leoni was unhappy and so was Alex.

"Well, one day she must have snapped. That's what she's like, you see. She snaps suddenly. She came round to our house when no one was in, and she opened the door to my guinea-pig run which was in the back garden. One of my guinea pigs escaped, but the other one obviously didn't go out straight away. I found him much later trapped under the door. She not only opened the door, but she tore it off its bottom hinges so the door collapsed on top of the poor guinea pig. He must have died really slowly. He wasn't even properly dead when I got home. I tried to revive him and took him to the vet's and everything, but it was too late. I've never seen the other guinea pig since, but he won't have been able to survive in the wild."

"How did you find out that she was the one who did it?" I asked.

"Because one of the neighbours was hanging out her washing and she saw her in our garden through a hole in the hedge. She saw a girl opening the door to the run and just thought it was a friend of mine who'd come to feed them because I'd asked her to. I asked her to describe what the girl looked like and she'd specially noticed the shoes. Well, you know Evi's shoes. No one wears shoes like Evi's, do they?"

I knew what he meant.

"Why should she do such a horrible thing?" I asked, knitting my eyebrows.

"Because she desperately wants to be some-one's best friend," Alex said. "But she can't bear it if that person has any other friends. That's why she punished George. And now she's getting desperate. Goodness knows what she'll do to the next person she gets her claws into."

"She's already got her claws into me," I admitted softly. "A lot of things have fallen into place from what you've just told me," I added, looking round the table. "She's ruined my project, she's stolen my best friend's money and tried to pin it on me … and worst of all she deliberately frightened the life out of me in my own house, at night time, when I was on my own."

The other three gasped when I said that. I couldn't believe it myself, except that I *had* to believe it. Then I suddenly remembered some-thing and I felt sick.

"You know the other day when you were in here and we were all sitting over there, with Tash's little sister?" I said to Leoni.

"Yes, and Claws was sitting over there by the door," Leoni replied.

"Well, I don't suppose you happened to see what went on, did you?"

"What do you mean?" asked Alex.

"I've got the horrible feeling that Evi might have encouraged Tash's little sister, Peta, to go out of the café all on her own when you two were just about to go and you'd got the door open. Peta kept insisting that it was Evi who'd 'put her out', but we all thought she was getting mixed up."

"I wouldn't put it past Evi," Alex said. "I really wouldn't. That girl is capable of anything. I dread to think what she'll do to the next person she gets her claws into," she repeated, shaking her head slowly.

My blood ran cold. I suddenly remembered about the hard look that Fen had seen on Evi's face. She *must* have overheard Tash talking. Omigod! Tash was in deep trouble.

"Sorry, I've just realized something terrible. I've got to go," I gabbled, as I lunged into the kitchen, grabbed Andy, dragged her back to our table and gave Andy, Fen and Leah a very fast account of some of the evil things Evi had done. I didn't tell them everything because I didn't want to waste time.

Fen immediately reacted the same way I had.

"Omigod! Tash! Come on, we've got to go and rescue her!"

Andy couldn't leave until she'd finished work, but we all knew she'd be joining us later. As for the rest of us, I don't think we've ever left the café quite so fast.

"Good luck!" Alex called out from table four.

"Thanks," I called back.

I only glanced quickly at their table, but I got good vibes from all of them. Isn't it amazing? I thought. Ten minutes before, I was convinced that Leoni and Alex hated my guts, and George and Pete were big bullies.

How wrong I was!

Chapter 7

The nearer we got to Tash's, the worse Fen's state became.

"I wish we'd never set eyes on that Evi Bligh," she said, but we could hardly make her words out because she was completely puffed from running. We all were.

"Yeah, why did she have to come to our school, anyway?" Leah added, quite aggressively for her.

"She said it was because of her dad's job, but now I wonder whether they moved because she was really unpopular or something," I said.

Nobody spoke after that until we got into Tash's drive.

"We could be wrong about everything, you know," Leah suddenly said, which made Fen and I stare at her in amazement.

"I mean, we haven't got any proof about anything, have we?"

"There's my project for a start," I said.

"But there's no actual *proof* that Evi was responsible for that, is there?"

"But what about everything that Pete and George said?"

"They may be lying."

"Leah, you're joking. They wouldn't lie about something like that."

"How do you know?"

I couldn't believe what I was hearing. I looked at Fen for help. I knew I could rely on Fen because it was her best friend who was at risk at the moment.

"We'll soon find out, won't we?" Fen said, simply. "Come on! Let's go and see."

"What if she's not here?" Leah asked in a whisper.

"Somebody's sure to be here because of Peta," Fen pointed out.

We knocked on the back door and waited. Personally I was praying that it wouldn't be Peta who answered the door, because although she can be very entertaining, the last thing you want is Peta entertaining you when you're in a hurry.

Unfortunately, my prayer was not answered.

"Hello, you silly billies!" Peta greeted us with an enormous beam. "What's you lot all doin' at my house?"

"Is Tash here?" Fen asked, getting straight to the point.

"I fink so," answered Peta, knitting her eyebrows together then wiggling them. She'd obviously only just discovered what it felt like to move your eyebrows about.

"Can we come in?" Leah asked.

"If you wipe your feet proper or take your shoes off more like," Peta grudgingly condescended.

None of us was in the mood for joking or any form of lightheartedness, so we all just kicked off our shoes and more or less pushed past Peta.

"I fink Tasher Basher is hiding, actually," she then informed us, which did not impress us. Leah, Fen and I all exchanged glances of *Oh dear! Peta is in one of those moods, is she?*

"Is that girl Evi with her?" I asked softly.

"No," replied Peta, in an even softer voice, widening her eyes and looking furtively around her as though this was all part of a very exciting game.

"I'll go up to Tash's room," Fen said, obviously having decided she'd had enough.

"She isn't hiding in her room," Peta informed us, "but you *can* look there if you want – just to see."

Fen took a deep breath and seemed as though she was about to speak sharply, but then changed her mind, because in the long run it was always safer to keep on the right side of Peta.

"OK, I'll go and see," Fen responded, and off she went up the stairs, two at a time.

110

She was down in under half a minute.

"Look, Peta, this is very important. Is Tash here or not? And if not, *who* is looking after you?"

At that point a door opened upstairs and Danny came down, looking tired.

"Tash's gone to the dentist," he said wearily. "I'm revising. I only wish I could go to the dentist too. It'd beat physics any day."

Leah's look said, *See, I told you there was nothing to worry about.*

"Was a girl called Evi Bligh here?" I asked.

"Oh, that's her name, is it?" said Danny, looking as though we were discussing a dead fly.

I waited for him to go on.

"She went," he said simply.

"Do you know where?" I asked.

"Haven't got a clue."

We were about to turn away when we all heard the distinct sound of a car pulling up. Danny looked out of the window.

"Mum's back."

Tash's mum, Helen, came in, looking fed up.

"Why are there always delays at dentists?" she asked in an exasperated voice, before she noticed us. "Oh, hello, you lot. I've left Tash there." She turned to Danny. "I'll relieve you of Peta, then you can get on in peace."

"OK, thanks, Mum," said Danny, turning slowly to go upstairs and finish his revision.

"Do you know where Evi went?" I asked Helen.

"I've no idea. She was going to work with Tash on their project, but Tash had completely forgotten about her dental appointment. How's your mum, Jaimini?"

"Oh, she's all right at the moment, thanks. She just has to take it really easy."

"I'll go and see her early next week. I've been thinking about her so much."

I smiled at Helen. She was such a lovely warm person. Like Tash, really.

"Actually, I may be wrong, but I'm not sure that Tash and Evi parted on the best of terms."

"Why? What happened?" I asked quickly.

"Well, I wasn't really listening, but I think Evi may have decided to do her project with someone else. I must admit, I couldn't quite work out why Tash wasn't doing it with *you*, Fen."

"Well, it's quite a long story," Fen said.

"Oh well, I'd better get back to the dentist. Where's Peta gone now?"

So we said goodbye to Helen and were about to go off home, when something suddenly occurred to me. I stood stock-still.

"Luce!"

"What? Where?" asked Leah, looking all around her.

"I bet that's where Evi's gone! Luce's!"

"But why?" asked Fen.

"Because that's the way she operates. Tash has let her down. That's why she had the argument with her. You must have been right about Evi overhearing what you and Tash said during games, Fen. Evi knew Tash was going to drop her the moment the project was finished, so she had to go for someone else. She knows that Luce and I aren't exactly the best of friends at the moment so I bet you anything she's gone to Luce's. She's probably there right now. Let's go. Come on."

The other two looked at each other, as if they thought I'd lost my marbles or something, but they came with me anyway. For some reason or other they had seemed much more concerned when they'd thought that Tash was in danger of being at Claws' mercy, than now, when Luce obviously was.

As we approached Luce's house I began to feel a bit nervous. I hadn't seen Melanie since that day outside the newsagent's, and she might not be too pleased with me, seeing as I'd lied to her about Dad being at home.

We knocked on the door and I felt even more nervous. Fen and Leah didn't know anything about all the happenings of the other night, and neither did they know any details of what had actually gone wrong between Luce and me. What if Luce and Evi were sitting happily working together? I could hardly go rushing in and break up the happy twosome by telling Luce that Evi was a nasty piece of work to be avoided at all costs. I mean, Luce probably thought that about *me*! I was beginning to feel more than a touch uneasy about having come here in the first place. Half of me wanted to turn round and go home, but the other half was so worried about what might have happened to Luce that I just couldn't go away now. I took a deep breath as the door opened.

"Hello, girls," said Melanie. "This is a surprise."

"Is Luce here?" I asked, giving Melanie my best smile. She gave me an *only-just* smile back.

"She's working on her project in the kitchen."

"Is Evi Bligh here, too?" I then asked, plucking up every ounce of courage I had.

Melanie's face clouded over. I definitely didn't imagine it. She looked irritated by my question.

"No, not at the moment," was the unexpected reply. We trooped through to the kitchen to find Luce deep into some work at the kitchen table. She looked up and couldn't disguise her obvious surprise at the sight of us lot in her kitchen.

For a moment we all just stood there and I felt stupid and tongue-tied. I wished Melanie would go out of the kitchen, then we could talk more freely. Luce's expression had turned to a slightly impatient one.

"The thing is, I've just been talking with those two boys…" I began, because I had to begin somewhere.

"What two boys?" Luce asked.

"You know, the one I told you about who I saw pushing Evi about and the other one who was sort of keeping watch?"

"Oh, them."

"Yes. They were in the café, you see, and they paid Andy with a ten-pound note and it had a red splodge on it, like the one that was stolen from you."

Melanie had had her back to us, and she was icing something, but she stopped and turned round at that point, then listened with her head on one side and an intense expression on her face.

"So, it was *them* who nicked my tenner! I'm not surprised. Evi's been telling me about them, and they sound horrible."

"No, you've got it wrong, Luce. Evi's been lying. *She* was the one who stole the tenner, then she gave it to George."

"Gave it to George! Why?"

"To stop him from telling anyone about why he and Pete were so angry with her that day."

"But they told you anyway."

"Yeah, because I was accusing them of stealing your tenner, and you weren't friends with me and I had to do something."

"So you're saying," said Melanie, in a rather hard voice that she never usually had, "that you watched two boys beating up that poor girl and didn't do anything about it? And now you actually believed them when they gave you some cock and bull story about Evi?"

Melanie looked really uptight. I was feeling more and more uncomfortable, yet I knew I was right.

"No, Evi was lying, honestly."

I looked at Fen and Leah for help but they'd both developed a massive fascination for the pattern on Melanie's kitchen floor tiles all of a sudden.

"Well, we all tell the occasional lie, don't we, Jaimini?" came Melanie's cold reply. The look she was levelling at me made me feel about four centimetres tall.

"Oh Mum, don't go on," said Luce, looking as embarrassed as I felt.

Fen and Leah had tuned in again because here was something they didn't know about and it was obvious from the enquiring expressions on their faces that they thought someone ought to fill them in. Thank goodness nobody did, but all the same I knew I was losing points. Leah was already unsure about the whole thing, and now that she was hearing I'd obviously told a lie that was serious enough to make Melanie lose her cool, she must have been getting highly suspicious about me.

Melanie had obviously decided that she'd better leave the room before she got too heavy, because she suddenly mumbled something about checking on Luce's eight-year-old twin brothers, and went out quickly. The relief I felt was enormous. I knew I had to tell Luce something that would make her see sense, and I had to do it quickly, before Melanie came back.

"Look, Luce, you've just got to believe me, those boys weren't lying. Evi wrenched off the door to George's guinea-pig run and one guinea pig escaped and the other one got stuck under what was left of the door and died."

"I'm not surprised she did that. I'd do that too if someone beat me up."

I was about to say that this was *before* they pushed her when Fen suddenly said, "Where *is* Evi, anyway?"

"She's taken Harry for a walk," Luce answered.

"But what if she harms him?" I asked, feeling aghast.

Why was nobody worried except me? They all looked so calm. In fact, worse than that, they looked as though they thought I was going totally over the top about Evi. Harry, by the way, is Luce's beloved dog. He was a stray who followed her home one day and she didn't like him at first, but she's finished up by loving him to distraction. I just know that if anything ever happened to Harry, Luce wouldn't be able to handle it.

"Of course she won't harm him," Luce snapped.

My brain was spinning around violently, trying to think of things I could say that would prove once and for all that Evi was not to be trusted.

"Look!" I said, pulling my project from my school bag. "She did this, too."

"How do you know?" asked Luce, simply.

"Well, I…"

By now all three of them were looking at me as though they really pitied me for being so small-minded.

"And that cookery competition…" I went on, groping for things to try to prove my point. "Kevin said it was Andy who said about you not entering. It was Andy who told him that I'd said it originally, but I never did, I swear. So I asked Andy and she said that Leah told her that I'd said it. And Leah said that Fen told *her*. So who told *you*, Fen?" I asked her, feeling desperate for her to give me the right answer. She did.

"I think it was Tash."

"Exactly. And who do you think told Tash?" I looked around triumphantly. Surely this proved my point. Why were they all looking so unimpressed?

"Who do *you* think told Tash?" Luce asked me.

"Well, Evi, of course."

This time nobody made any secret of the fact that they thought I was barking up the wrong tree. The three of them exchanged looks that made me feel a real outsider. I was about to launch into what had happened the night I'd been on my own when I realized that it was pointless. Whatever I said now would make the situation worse, not better. They wouldn't believe me, and it wasn't really any wonder. I was stuck. Totally stuck.

Leah suddenly looked at her watch.

"Is that the time? God, I'd better go."

"Yeah, me too," Fen added.

They both slipped out of the back door, saying bye to Luce as casually as they could, but I knew that the moment they got out of the door they'd be talking about how weirdly I was acting, saying all those nasty things about Evi. I couldn't believe the way Fen had changed her tune. It was all because of Leah. Well, that and Melanie's reaction to me.

Luce began colouring something in on her project, which gave me the slightest of hints that perhaps she wanted me to go. Just before I went, though, I wanted to know one thing.

"How long has Evi been gone with Harry?"

"Not very long. About…" Luce looked at her

watch and I saw her eyes widen. She quickly tried to look normal again, but I could tell she was a little bit alarmed, "...three quarters of an hour."

"Did she say where she was going?"

"No, she just said she knew a lovely place to take him. Look, Jaimini, Evi loves dogs. You should have seen her with Harry. And Harry liked her too, I could tell."

I didn't say any more. I had decided what I was going to do. I was going to look for Evi and Harry. I had the horrible feeling that Evi was about to put Harry in danger, then rescue him herself to get into Luce's good books. I thought back to Tash and Peta in the café. Evi had put Peta's life in danger, for goodness' sake, just so that she could rush out dramatically and rescue her. Of course, it had worked brilliantly because after that Tash was eternally grateful to her, and clever old Evi found herself a really nice new friend. But Tash must have realized what Evi was really like, only being Tash, she was too nice to drop Evi like a ton of bricks. She wanted to drop her gently, so as not to be unkind.

And now, here was the same scenario all over again, only this time with Luce and her beloved dog. What Evi had done to George was different. That was a punishment for the wrong she felt he'd done to her. She hadn't even intended George to know it was her. The only reason he found out was because the neighbour had just happened to be in the garden at that very time that Evi had been carying out her atrocious deed.

As I stood outside Luce's house, wondering whether to go one way towards the Terraced Gardens, which is a very popular park area, or another and make for the rec, I spotted a small figure running in my direction. I was pretty sure it was Andy. It was certainly running hard enough to be Andy. I stood still and waited. After a moment, my suspicions were confirmed. She waved and I waved back, then a few seconds later she came right up to me. Only Andy can run as hard as that and hardly get puffed out at all.

"Hi, I came to help," she said, turning her big eyes on me. "Where are the others?"

"Gone, because they don't think I've got it right about Evi."

"What! They must be mad! I've just been talking to Kevin. He told me that this blonde girl, who sounded exactly like Evi when he described her, came up to him today and asked him to reconsider about not counting Luce's first round entry in the cookery competition. She said that Luce was really cut up about it, and all sorts of people were deliberately not entering now because they felt sorry for Luce. Kevin said he took an instant dislike to the girl without even knowing why. He was only telling me about the conversation because he wondered if I knew who she was. I said I had a pretty good idea."

"How could she have seen him today, though? She wasn't in the café just now."

"That's exactly what *I* wondered, but Kevin said it was at about three o'clock so she must have sneaked out of school during games. Don't worry, it was definitely her because Kevin did an imitation and he did that thing where she puts her head on one side and bites her thumb nail. Kevin didn't half look funny, I can tell you!"

I couldn't believe what I was hearing, but thank goodness I'd at least got Andy on my side.

"How did you know to come to Luce's house when we'd said we'd be at Tash's?"

"I didn't know. It was just a hunch I had. When Kevin told me that Evi had started madly defending Luce for no apparent reason I figured that she'd probably decided to get her claws into *her* now so I came straight here to find out."

"The thing I'm not sure about," I began thoughtfully, "is whether Evi is trying to befriend Luce because she knows Tash is going to drop her, or because she wants to get at me. I know she hates my guts. I've got tons of proof."

I couldn't decide whether or not to tell Andy about what happened that night I was on my own. In the end I decided not to risk it, just in case she didn't believe me. As we walked along in the direction of the Terraced Gardens I explained that Evi had set off about three quarters of an hour before to take Harry on a walk, and still hadn't returned. Andy started to run when I said that but I couldn't keep up with her so she slowed down to a jog for my benefit.

We scoured the Terraced Gardens and twice we thought we'd seen her, but then realized that we'd been mistaken.

"It's no good, she could be anywhere," I said despondently.

"She's probably gone to the rec," said Andy.

"Oh no, that's miles away," I said wearily. Then an even more depressing thought struck me. "What if she's back with Luce? I bet she is, and we've just been wasting our time, and I'm going to look an even bigger idiot now."

"Look, Jaimini, *I* know you're right about Evi. *I'll* back you up. Even if we don't get her this time, we're sure to get her sometime."

Andy was so positive about everything. The biggest difference between us is that she doesn't let other people's opinions or actions get in the way of what she thinks. I made a resolution to try and be as positive as Andy, no matter what happened.

"I'm going to the rec," she said next. "You stay here and have one more look round."

"Yes, but I'd better make it a very quick look,

123

because Mum'll be on her own soon," I said, looking at my watch.

"OK, and I'll phone you at home if I've got any news."

She ran off like a lizard, darting quickly and smoothly between the strolling people. I let my eyes scan the park in every direction, but there were only two people with dogs that I could see, and they were both men, so I decided to give up, because I didn't want Mum left on her own again.

The quickest way to our house was to cut through a wooded area at the back of the park. Mum doesn't like me going through there on my own, but it saves so much time, and anyway, it wasn't dark or anything. I glanced up at the sky. There were a few clouds gathering, but I reckoned it wouldn't rain for a while, so I headed for the dark trees.

Twice, as I walked through the wood, I thought I heard a noise behind me, but each time I turned round there was nothing there. I told myself to stop listening so hard because I was getting myself into an unnecessary state of fear. After all, I reasoned, woods *do* have creaks and snaps and rustles, don't they? So the next time I heard a noise, I made myself keep walking and not look back. If only I *had* looked back.

If *only* I had.

Chapter 8

"Ow!" I screeched. "My back! Ow!"

I turned round and there stood Evi Bligh, grinning. I froze, but only for a second. The pain in my back was too much for me to stay still.

"What have you done, Evi, you stupid idiot?" I cried, as I writhed about.

"The nettle torture," she answered, still grinning.

It crossed my mind that she must be mad. She'd stuffed a big handful of nettles down my back and the pain was unbearable. I dropped my bag and tried to pull the back of my shirt out of my skirt so the nettles would drop out, but with every second that I was fumbling the nettles were stinging me agonizingly. Some of them fell out but the others wouldn't move, and when I tried to pull them I had to stop because it hurt my hands too much. Evi wore gloves, I noticed.

"Evi, *do* something! I'm in agony!"

"I'll get you some dock leaves. Come with me."

I couldn't believe this girl.

"No, just get these nettles out, for God's sake!"

"You'd better come with me, I think, otherwise you'll suffer even more."

I didn't know whether she meant that she had something else even worse in store for me, if I didn't do as she said, or whether she meant that unless I came with her, the nettles would have to stay down my back and that would make me suffer even more. By this time I was near to tears. I don't think I've ever experienced such pain.

We were going deeper into the wooded area instead of keeping to the path as I usually did, and I really couldn't go on because the nettles had slipped a bit so that the bottom of my back was getting stung.

"Here we are. These dock leaves will do the trick," Evi announced chirpily, and then I really *did* think she was mad. Suddenly, I made a decision. I pulled off my school jumper and then my shirt, and dropped them on the ground. One of the nettles must have got caught in my bra strap but I *had* to get it out because the pain was excruciating. By the time I'd managed to remove it, my right hand was stinging and throbbing, too. At that moment I was much more angry with Evi than I was scared of her. I found myself yelling at her hysterically.

"Rub those dock leaves on my back, Evi, or I'll see to it that everyone, and I mean *everyone*, gets to hear what a poor, pathetic, cruel person you really are!"

"And if I *do* rub the dock leaves on your back?"

I didn't know what to say, because I hated her so much that I knew I'd tell everyone about her anyway. On the other hand I was in agony and I knew I wouldn't make it home unless she did something. I felt so powerless, not being able to reach the middle of my back myself.

"You're not answering the question, Jaimini. Is it because you don't know the answer? I thought you knew the answer to everything, you're supposed to be so clever."

"For God's sake, rub my back, Evi, otherwise you'll be in big trouble."

I tried to sound threatening, but because I was so close to tears, I probably sounded weak and feeble.

"OK, turn round," she said simply, then she very gently began to flick the dock leaves over my back, but because she wasn't rubbing them in hard, if anything it made my back hurt even more.

"Harder!" I screamed at her.

"*Making Waves* by Jaimini Riva," came her strange answer. She had really shocked me this time. How did Evi know the title of my story? Nobody except Mum and Dad and Mrs Merle had read my story.

"What! What did you say?" My voice was scarcely more than a whisper as I slowly turned to face her.

"'When the noise finally stopped, it shocked Mr Zeta so much that he dropped the glass he was holding so it shattered into hundreds of tiny pieces, and made its own small impact on the silence…'"

"How do you know my story? Where did you read that?" I asked her, my temper mounting.

She was beginning to walk backwards away from me, in the direction that we'd come from, back towards the park. She still wore that awful grin. I stayed rooted to the spot and the pain in my back seemed less now, but only because I was too cross to feel hurt.

"I read it at school one day," she answered, still walking away from me.

"You can't have done," I shouted, knowing that this was a stupid thing to say, because she'd proved that she *had* read it by quoting the first sentence.

"I found it in the school office, in a brown envelope, all ready to be posted."

"You went into the school office?"

"I chose my moment carefully, and I was only

in there for a few seconds. I'd heard Mrs Merle say she was going to post it for you, then I waited till she came out of the staffroom next, and I saw that she had it with her, so I followed her to the school office, where she left it in the pile of letters for posting. Easy!"

I was beginning to feel weak. This could not be happening.

"What did you do with it when you'd read it?" I shouted out because she'd moved even further away by then.

"Put it back in the envelope and re-sealed it, of course," she called back.

Relief flowed through my body, but I still felt weak and tembly.

"Just one slight adjustment, though. I changed the entry form so it read Evi Bligh, not Jaimini Riva. It wasn't difficult with all that Tipp-Ex in the office. In fact, there was so much Tipp-Ex that I thought they wouldn't miss one little bottle."

The trembling in my limbs got worse and I fell backwards against a tree. I looked down, but only for a few seconds because I'd lost my footing. When I looked back up, she was out of sight. My heart started to race as I jerked my head this way and that to check she wasn't going to suddenly appear from somewhere else.

I shivered and realized I was standing in the middle of a wood with no shirt and no jumper on.

My back was boiling hot but the rest of me was cold. I reached down for my shirt, and then the horrible realization hit me. Evi had taken my shirt and jumper. She'd obviously stuffed them in her school bag. That was why she'd been moving away from me, so she could get a head start when I started to run after her.

Oh, what a stupid, stupid situation to be in! I couldn't go home now, not like this, with only my bra on the top half. An awful despair was beginning to seep into every pore of my body and I knew I was about to burst into tears, especially when I looked at my watch and saw to my horror that it was just gone seven o'clock. Mum would be on her own now because Dad wasn't coming home till eight-thirty. I covered my eyes with my hands, then quickly took them away again because for all I knew, Evi Bligh might have been watching me from some hiding place or other. That girl really did need help.

I searched through my own school bag, even though I knew it was pointless because there wasn't any games kit or anything like that in there. I swallowed hard, and told myself to be positive like Andy. Right, so what would Andy do in this situation? I thought for a moment, and decided that she'd probably just walk home in her bra and ignore people's stares.

Did I dare to do that? Perhaps if I carried my

school bag in my arms, instead of slinging it on my shoulder, that would cover most of me. It would just be the back that would look funny. Come to think about it, the back would look horrific because it was probably totally red with nettle rash all over it. The awful stinging sensation was still there, but just then it seemed like the least of my worries.

Maybe I should go back to the park and approach the first person I saw, and explain that someone had played a practical joke on me and ask them ... and ask them what? In two seconds flat all that positive feeling had gone out of me. I couldn't even sit down because the ground was dirty and covered in twigs and leaves. So I just stood there and hung my head and wished that I could wake up and find it was all a bad dream.

A moment later my head shot back up again, though, because I realized that someone was approaching me. There was a definite noise of footsteps and someone was calling out but I couldn't make out what they were calling.

I crossed my hands over my chest and hunched my shoulders, praying that this was Andy or one of the others, but as the voice got louder, I realized it was Luce, and she was calling out to Harry, her dog.

"Luce!" I called back, but not very loudly because I was cold, scared and embarrassed.

"Jaimes! Omigod!" As she stumbled towards me, she was ripping off her jumper. It's funny the things you remember, isn't it? The thing that stayed in my mind more than anything about this moment was that Luce's hair was sticking out like a halo because of all the static electricity in her school jumper. She was pulling it down over my head and as my arms went through the sleeves and she dragged it down my back I winced in pain.

"Oh Jaimes, whatever's happened?" Without waiting for an answer she spun me round, lifted the jumper and said "Omigod!" three times.

"Did *she* do this to you?" she asked through clenched teeth.

I nodded.

"I'll kill her. Come on. My place is nearer than yours. You need to get some Anthisan on there."

"What about Harry?" I asked, as she set off back in the direction from which she'd come at about a hundred miles an hour, dragging me by the hand as though she was the mother and I was the naughty child. That's the wonderful thing about Luce: she doesn't go in for huge post mortems, she just carries on as though nothing's happened. I mean, we'd spent the last few days hating each other's guts, and here was Luce holding my hand and talking about Anthisan. I almost laughed it was so ridiculous.

"What are you smiling at?" she demanded.

"You. I'm just happy we're together again."

"Me too. That girl's got a lot to answer for."

"But what about Harry?" I repeated.

"I'll find him after I've got you safely back."

I knew Luce was worrying like mad about Harry. I could tell by the hard expression on her face. This was her way of dealing with her worry and sadness, to harden herself and get on with the matter in hand.

"Can I phone Mum from your place? She'll be all on her own."

"No, she's not on her own. Tash is staying with her until your dad gets back."

"Tash? How come?"

So as we half walked, half stumbled back to Luce's place she told me what had happened since I'd last seen her.

"After you'd gone I felt cross at first, because you seemed to have changed so much recently, and then there you were, coming out with all that stuff about Evi when I thought Evi was a perfectly nice girl. She told me why you didn't want to stay the night at our place. She was very embarrassed to tell me, but she told me anyway."

I interrupted Luce at this point. "But she doesn't even *know*!"

"She said you confessed to her that you weren't friends with me any more, then you begged her to stay the night at your place, so she did."

"And did you believe her?"

"I did at the time, yes. It all made sense."

"Well, she was lying, I swear! I spent the night on my own until Dad got back."

"I couldn't help believing her. She even described some of the rooms in your house, including your landing."

"That's because she *was* there. I left the back door unlocked by mistake. I can't tell you how scared I was. Well, you know I've always been afraid of the dark, and when I finally plucked up the courage to go to bed, I heard these noises from downstairs, and then they were *on* the stairs, and I put a chair under my door handle, but then the most horrific thing of all happened. I could hear this scratching on the other side of my door. I tell you, Luce, I was petrified."

"Oh Jaimes, I'm not surprised. I would have screamed the place down."

"I very nearly did. I just cowered there on the floor in my room, and after a few minutes I heard really loud noises, footsteps coming up the stairs, but not creeping or anything, walking normally. I nearly had a heart attack at that point, but it was Dad, thank goodness. I burst into tears I was so relieved."

"So what was that scratching noise?"

"Well, when I told Dad about it, he said that as

he drove up he saw a girl with blondish hair running away and she looked just like you. In fact, he thought it *was* you. Actually, he was so sure of himself that I began to believe he must be right. You can imagine how I felt then…"

"Oh Jaimes, what a terrible mix-up this whole thing has been!"

"But what made *you* change your mind about Evi, Luce?"

"Well, Tash turned up about twenty minutes after you'd gone."

"Tash?"

"Yes, she got her mum to drop her off at my place after the dentist's. She told me how Evi had suddenly turned nasty and refused to do the project with her. Apparently Evi said that Tash was mean and ungrateful considering she'd saved Peta's life. Only Tash knew differently because the hygienist from the dentist's had happened to be in the shop across the road from the café that day, and she asked Tash what on earth that strange-looking blonde girl was doing, forcing Tash's sister to go out of the café when the road was so dangerous. She said she was on the point of rushing over to get Peta out of danger when the blonde girl leapt to the rescue herself."

"So now we know just what depths she'll sink to," I said slowly.

"Before Tash went to the dentist's, she felt

really torn about Evi. Her gut reaction was that she didn't trust Evi at all, yet there was no getting away from the fact that this was the person who had apparently saved Peta's life. Poor Tash didn't know what to do. Fortunately, the big argument that was brewing between them got interrupted by Helen taking Tash off to see the dentist, but apparently just before Evi went, she told Tash that she knew someone who really wanted to do the project with her, someone who wasn't two-faced like Tash. That's what Evi said.

"While she was in the dentist's chair, Tash was feeling frantic, because she knew she had to warn the rest of us about her. When she'd told me all this I really started to worry because there was no sign of Evi or Harry. Then Andy turned up and filled me in on what Kevin had said, and I knew then that three of you couldn't be wrong.

"Actually I was really touched that you and Andy were out looking for *my* dog. It suddenly snapped me into action and made me join the search. Look, I'm really sorry about everything, Jaimes…"

Luce put her arm round my shoulder, forgetting about my back.

"Aargh!" I screeched.

"Oh, sorry… Oh no … quick! I'll get the Anthisan."

We'd reached her house and she legged it

upstairs and was down again in no time at all. It was as she was gently rubbing Anthisan into my back that Melanie came in and threw up her hands in horror and said she thought I ought to have an anti-histamine injection. I promised her I would, but first I had more important things to attend to. She didn't ask how it had happened, but Luce and her mother exchanged significant looks, and Melanie gave me a very warm, sympathetic smile, so I knew I was back in her good books again.

There was a knock on the door and there on the doorstep stood Andy, Fen and Leah!

"I phoned Fen and Leah and explained everything to them because I thought we needed reinforcements," said Andy.

"Look what *she* did to Jaimes," was Luce's unexpected reply.

With that she triumphantly showed them my back and when they'd all expressed total horror, I put one of Luce's shirts and jumpers on, and we got ready to leave, with Melanie talking about phoning the police about Harry.

Luce protested and said that the five of us would be better than the police, and I added that Tash would be joining us any second because my dad had just got home. I'd given Mum a quick ring to reassure her that I wouldn't be long and said I'd explain the whole thing when I got back.

She'd said that Tash had explained a fair amount, and that she hoped that nasty Evi girl got her come-uppance. Funny expression that, isn't it?

It wasn't until we were all heading towards the rec, after Tash had joined us and we'd talked through every detail of Evi's manipulative dealings, that we suddenly became subdued. After all, this wasn't an adventure. This was a search for Luce's beloved dog. What if we didn't find him? What if we *did* find him and he was...? It didn't bear thinking about.

"I thought you'd searched the rec, Andy?" I said.

"No, I changed my mind at the last minute and went up near that old dumping yard, because I thought the rec was too open and obvious for her to try anything ... nasty..."

"But why should she want to hurt Harry?" Luce asked, her eyes looking very green in her pale face all of a sudden.

"She's sick, that's why," Fen replied. The rest of us didn't say anything, but we all agreed.

"Do you think Mum was right? Would it be better if I reported Harry as missing?"

"Let's just try the rec, then if we still don't find him, we'll contact the police."

When we got there we decided to go off in twos because it was beginning to get a tiny bit dark, and Fen had once had an awful experience on the rec so she was quite scared to be on her own. Luce and I set off to the right, Andy and Leah to the left, and Fen and Tash went down the middle. Luce and I had copped the bit with the trees, and personally I was beginning to hate the sight of trees. My back was still throbbing and felt as though I'd got really bad sunburn, but compared to the agony I had been in, this was bliss. As we approached the wooded area I felt Luce tensing up.

"What?" I asked. "Did you hear something?"

"No, but I'm sure he's here. I can feel it."

I prayed that she was right and that Harry was alive and well. Still there was no sound.

"Harry," called Luce softly. "Harry!"

We both stood quite still to listen but there was no answering bark, not even a whine.

When we'd walked a little further, we went through the same process, then we walked on a bit and so on. By this time we'd gone past the trees and were on the open field.

"It's hopeless," Luce suddenly said. "We're never going to find him. Mum was right, I ought to call the police."

"Hang on a sec," I said, waving my hand at her to shut her up, because I was sure I'd heard something.

As we stood there, straining for the tiniest sound, the very silence seemed to be noisy. Just at that moment in time there wasn't a bird singing or a tree stirring. Then, into the silence came the distant, soulful whining of a dog. Luce's hand clutched my arm but still we didn't move a muscle. A few seconds later, it came again. This second time it seemed even quieter, but it was definitely a dog.

"Is it Harry?" I asked.

"I think so," Luce replied. "It was coming from over there, wasn't it?"

I nodded and we set of towards the row of houses which backed on to the rec a little distance away.

"It can't be Harry," said Luce despondently. "It must have been a dog that lives in one of those houses."

"But why should it be making that whining noise?" I asked, thinking as I spoke that it was probably a pretty stupid question because there could have been a hundred reasons why a dog might have been whining.

"Maybe it's shut in and it wants to go out," suggested Luce.

"Let's just check all the same," I said.

"So what do we do, go marching up to someone's front door and say, 'Excuse me, but I've lost my dog and I have reason to believe that you have stolen it, as I can distinctly hear a dog whining in this house'?"

She was right – it sounded stupid, and I was on the point of agreeing with her that perhaps we'd better call it a day, when once again the sad whine came to our ears, only this time much more loudly.

"It *is* Harry. I'm sure it's Harry! I'd know that sound anywhere," cried Luce, clutching my arm again with a bit more force this time.

We crept forwards, listening like mad all the time.

"Harry!" called Luce. "Harry, where are you?"

This time there was a small bark for an answer, and Luce actually smiled. "At least he's alive," she whispered.

The bark sounded as though it had come from the house with the messiest back garden. There were two small sheds – well, one of them was minute. Then there was an old blue plastic sand-pit with a warped lid that didn't quite fit, but it was weighed down by rain water. Next to that there was one of those circular bouncy things, but it was all rusty, and alongside that was an old wheelie bin with a little hole in it. All this lot were just the other side of a broken-down fence, but they were also in full view of every window at the back of the house.

"What a dump," Luce whispered.

"We can't go in. Someone's sure to see us," I pointed out.

"We'll have to," answered Luce. "It would take ages to go all the way round to the front."

She was right, of course. It was just that I was feeling chicken about trespassing, in case any dodgy-looking people got cross with us. No sooner had this thought crossed my mind, than a thin man in old jeans held up with a piece of string appeared from the back door. He didn't see us at first, but Harry chose that moment to bark quite loudly, which made the man look straight at us with a startled expression on his face.

"That your dog barking?" he asked roughly.

"Yes, I think so," Luce answered. "I think he might be in one of your sheds."

"One of my sheds? How in the world did he land up in one of my sheds? I keep 'em shut, these sheds."

"I don't really know, because someone else took him out for a walk, you see, and she doesn't like me now, so she was probably trying to…"

While Luce had been attempting some sort of an explanation the man had been totally ignoring her, but was putting a lot of energy into tugging at the handle of one of the sheds.

"Well, he ain't in there. Let's try this one."

He then opened the other tiny shed without any problem. "And he ain't in there, either."

"He's not in the sandpit, is he?" I asked, feeling worried.

"What, squashed flat as a pancake?" the man asked, grinning, and showing a lot of rotten teeth as he flung off the sandpit lid with great effort because the rain water had accumulated in a pool and must have made the lid heavy.

"Ssh," the man then ordered, even though we weren't making a sound. Harry had gone back to his whining, and the man was very slowly inching towards the old wheelie bin, with his head on one side and his eyebrows knitted together.

"Well, bless me! Look at this," he said, grinning once again and beckoning to us to join him. We didn't need to be told twice. We shot through that fence in no time at all, and squatted down beside him.

"Poor little blighter," the man said, and Luce and I found ourselves face to face with Harry's wet nose which was poking out of the hole in the wheelie bin.

"Oh Harry!" said Luce, with a quaver in her voice as Harry's tongue came out and he licked her cheek.

The man carefully turned the bin on its side, which made the lid drop open, and out crept a very subdued-looking Harry, who laid his head against Luce as she stroked him and talked to him in a voice so soft that I couldn't make out her words at all.

"The old fella's pleased to see you then," commented the man, still grinning as he pulled out a piece of long grass and started chewing it. "How he found his way into that bin is a mystery, though."

Luce took a deep breath and opened her mouth to speak, but I gave her a very discreet shake of the head, which was supposed to say, Don't bother, Luce. So she just said, "Yeah. It's a mystery."

"A mystery," I added.

Long after we'd left the man's garden, with Harry walking obediently between us, we looked back and saw that the man hadn't moved at all. With his hands in his pockets, he was staring at the bin, which still lay on its side.

"Actually, he's right, it *is* a mystery," I said to Luce. "How on earth did Evi manage to lift Harry up and put him in the bin? She couldn't have done it on her own."

"She's so devious she probably turned the bin on its side, then heaved it up when Harry was inside."

Luce frowned, then we turned back and could just make out four distant figures heading in our direction, so we waved like mad, and watched them all break into a run. It was Andy and the others. They must have spotted Harry.

Chapter 9

We were all so high on the relief and happiness of getting Harry back safe and sound that it wasn't till the following afternoon when we were all at the café together that we actually gave Evi a thought. It was Saturday and Luce was on duty but she was having a typical Luce-type pause at our table.

"Lucky for Evi it's not a school day today," Fen commented.

"What's the betting she'll skive on Monday?" said Luce vehemently.

"She can't skive for ever," Andy pointed out. "We'll get her sooner or later."

"I bet she's really sweating," added Fen.

"For all we know, she may have been watching us yesterday evening when we went off with Harry," Tash said thoughtfully.

We contemplated this in silence for a few seconds, then it was Andy who spoke.

"I reckon Tash is right about that. That would be exactly Evi's style, wouldn't it? I was just thinking about what she did to poor little Peta. She doesn't care *what* she does. She'll do anything to draw attention to herself, she's so desperate for friends."

"*Is* she desperate for friends, or does she get some kind of weird buzz out of breaking up friendships?" Leah asked, frowning.

"I think that breaking up friendships is the only way she knows of getting friends," I said.

"Jaimes is right," said Fen. "I bet she couldn't believe it when we actually managed to track down Harry by ourselves. She was probably just waiting for the moment when we all gave in, then she would have flown to the rescue, and hey presto! Once again she would have had someone eating out of her hand. Only in this case it would have been Luce."

"I don't think she really wanted to be my friend, you know," Luce remarked. "I think she picked me because she's always had it in for Jaimes."

"Why? Why me?" I asked protestingly.

It was Fen who answered. "Because, one: you're brainier than her, and she's jealous…"

"It's true, she once *did* say something that made me think she was jealous of that," I said thoughtfully.

146

"And two: you entered a competition that *she* wanted to win," went on Fen.

I nodded and was about to tell them what had happened to my entry when I caught a quick look pass between Fen and Luce. It was a warning look. Luce was warning Fen about something. I know I didn't imagine it. It made me feel left out for a moment and brought back all the horrible memories of why Luce and I had broken off our friendship in the first place. I looked down and gave myself an extremely quick, extremely firm talking to. *Forget it, Jaimini. That's all history now. You're getting neurotic. Stop being silly!*

"And three," continued Fen, "*you* were the one who blew her cover. All the time she was dealing with the Georges and the Petes of this world, she knew she was OK because she could buy them off…"

"Where do you think she got all her money from then?" asked Tash.

"No idea. That's another of those mysteries. There are so many mysteries surrounding that girl…" Fen replied, "but to finish off what I was saying, Evi hadn't reckoned on Jaimini, or anyone, seeing George laying into her. She wasn't used to people interfering with her little schemes and making complications. It must have really bugged her when Jaimini tried to persuade her to report those boys."

"Back to work, young lady," said Jan, leaning over Luce. "Too much gossiping by far."

"Sorry," said Luce, jumping up and nearly knocking the tray that Jan was carrying out of her hands in the process.

Luce's going had the effect of making us wind up our conversation, and I never did tell the others how Evi had changed my entry form. We started playing a favourite game of ours. We all have to look round the café, find one person to focus on, and build a story round them, like how old they are, where they live, who with, what job they do, etc etc.

We were deep into this game when out of the corner of my eye I spotted a blonde girl by the door.

"Look!" I cried.

The others all started violently swinging round to see what I was looking at.

"What? What?"

"That was Evi, I'm sure!"

"Where?"

"Just outside. I'm sure it was her."

"So what are we waiting for?" Andy said, jumping up.

She was at the door before the rest of us had time to blink.

"You go with Andy, Jaimes," said Fen.

"OK."

I wasn't convinced that I'd be able to keep up with Andy but I didn't want to waste any more time because she was waiting at the door.

"This way, quick! I can just see her," she said, grabbing my arm once we were outside. Then she set off at her usual rapid speed.

The High Street was quite busy, but being little and agile, Andy just darted between people, and it wasn't long before a gap stretched between us. I tried my best to catch her up, but it was no good, and if anything the gap was widening. At one point she turned round and I saw her head bobbing this way and that, trying to see where I'd got to.

"You go on," I yelled, with a flick of my out-stretched arm. She obviously got the message because she turned immediately and shot off out of sight.

I began to make my way slowly back to the café, and it was then that I happened to glance across the road and felt sure I'd seen Evi disappearing into a shop. I stopped and stared, then impul-sively crossed the road and went into the same shop, which was a food market. There were three women talking just inside the door, and they didn't hear my timid, "Excuse me, please."

"Excuse me, please," I said more loudly, and eventually one of them clicked on that they were blocking the doorway, and slowly moved to one side. By the time I'd made my way down the aisle between the tinned foods and the frozen foods, then turned the corner and gone down the other aisle to the till, there was no sign of Evi.

Sighing, I went out, and this time I made it all the way back to the café without any further sightings. I could only hope that I'd been mistaken and that Andy would come back triumphant.

"Did you get her?" Luce asked, grabbing me the moment I walked through the door to the café.

"No, I couldn't keep up with Andy, so she's gone on alone... But Luce, what can she do? What can Andy actually *do* to Evi?"

"She can kill her," Luce answered, without changing her expression at all.

"No, be sensible, Luce."

"OK, she can point out to her that somehow we're going to get her back, and she can tell her what a sick girl she really is."

"Hm," was my only answer as I went over to the others who were beckoning me frantically. It was only about five minutes later that Andy returned, looking distinctly stressed.

"It wasn't her," she told us as she flopped into a chair.

"Thanks for trying, Andy," said Luce, leaning over impulsively and giving Andy a kiss. "Ugh! You're sweating," she added with distaste, gulping at Fen's lemonade and making a big thing of licking it over her lips, which at least had the effect of breaking our sombre mood for a moment.

Incredibly, two weeks went by, and not once did anyone set eyes, even for a second, on Evi Bligh. Apparently a neighbour of Luce's, an old lady called Mrs Stone, said she saw a shifty-looking blonde girl wandering around Luce's back garden and looking in her shed one time when there was no one in at Luce's house.

"It's her!" Luce had said, her green eyes glinting. "She's still trying to get Harry. I can't ever relax."

We had asked two or three teachers where Evi was, but they all said the same thing: "She's rather poorly." Funny expression, that, isn't it?

"Skiving, more like," Luce muttered each time, and we all agreed with her.

Then Luce got some great news. She came rushing in one morning to tell us that she'd made it to the final of the cookery competition. There were three finalists and they all had to cook their dish for the final round in the kitchen of the café. Then Martin Rhuanna would taste all three dishes and make his decision. The grand announcement was to be made in the café itself.

After all the discussion about whether or not Luce should be allowed to enter the competition because of her mother being a caterer, it was decided by Jan that this was all nonsense, and "Of course Luce can enter." She pointed out the very obvious fact that everyone else seemed to have overlooked, that anyone might have a mum or dad or whoever who could help them, and just because Luce's mum happened to be a caterer, it didn't make her the best cook in the country. Also, as she quite rightly said, all the cooking for the competition was done either at school for the first round, or in the café kitchen for the final round, so there was no way anyone could cheat in those circumstances.

"When is it, Luce?" asked Tash excitedly.

"Thursday," answered Luce happily. "Help! Only two days."

"Who else has got through to the final?" Leah asked. "Anyone we know?"

"I've no idea," Luce answered, so we all rushed down to the café after school that day, and even though it was Leah's turn on duty, the whole lot of us went in through the back door to the kitchen.

"Oh, no! Girls! Girls!" cried Kevin, putting his hands in front of his face as though protecting himself from millions of fans, like a big pop star or something. "No, no! I'll give autographs, but please don't rip my clothes off!"

"Oh, shut up, Kevin," Fen said.

"Don't you tell me to shut up, Nelly," Kevin

responded, pretending to be seriously cross.

"Kevin, you've got to tell us," Fen went on. "Who else is in the cookery final with Luce?"

"Yes, where is that clever girl?" said Kevin, then he gave Luce a kiss on each cheek, French fashion, and said with a strong French accent, "Congrrratulation, ma cherrrrie. You 'ave done verrry verrry well to become one of zee sreee eencrrrredible finaleeeests!"

"But who are the other two?" Luce asked, gripping Kevin's shoulders in an attempt to stop him from going back to his cooking.

"Give those pans a stir," he threw over his shoulder to the rest of us, then he leant forwards and whispered into Luce's ear.

We all waited patiently as Leah and I gave a token stir without looking what we were doing. The way Luce's eyes went huge and round and her jaw dropped open couldn't have escaped the notice of the least observant person on the planet and we all waited to hear what Kevin had said.

"You're joking!" Luce breathed.

"Why should I joke? What's the big deal about Evi Bligh?"

At the sound of the dreaded name the rest of us all gasped and it was a good job Kevin took over the stirring because Leah and I had come to a standstill, we were so shocked.

"Evi Bligh!" Andy exclaimed. "She's the one

you told me about, Kevin! You know, the one who said that Luce should be allowed to enter the competition after all."

"Oh, her!" Kevin said. "Yes, come to think about it, Martin was very impressed by her cooking in the first round. Sorry, girls, but she must be good if Martin says so."

"So you mean … she'll be … here the day after tomorrow, then?" I said slowly, thinking ahead.

"Yup. Two o'clock."

At that we all looked at each other and broke into grins of delight.

"What makes me think there are six girls in here who all want to see Evi Bligh at two o'clock the day after tomorrow?" Kevin asked, raising his eyebrows for a moment.

"You're not kidding," Fen replied for us all.

"Who's the other finalist?" I asked Luce.

"Who did you say it was, Kevin?" Luce asked.

"Jonathan Weekes."

None of us lot had ever heard of Jonathan Weekes, but one thing was certain, even if we had to skive off school, we would *all* be at the café at two o'clock on Thursday afternoon.

"You've *got* to beat her, Luce," said Tash, looking as hard as Tash ever looks.

"Yes, you've *got* to," we all agreed, then we went into the café, leaving Leah to get on with the washing-up.

* * *

On Thursday something happened that none of us could have anticipated. During assembly, Ms Chambers, our Head, announced that the results of the literary competition had arrived and there was to be a ceremony to make the very special announcement – that afternoon at two o'clock.

Immediately we all looked at each other and our eyes flashed signs of *Oh no! We want to be at the café for Luce but we also want to be at school to hear who's won the literary comp.*

The moment assembly was over we all gathered in the corridor, and it was then that I told them how Evi had changed the entry form with my story so it looked as though *she* had written the story.

The way they all reacted you'd think I'd just announced that I'd married an African warrior chief and was about to spend the rest of my life in a mud hut. They just stared at me open-mouthed, then Tash, the first to collect her wits, spoke.

"But why didn't you tell us before?"

I couldn't answer her question without opening up old wounds so I didn't answer at all, just shrugged.

"The thing is," I said, "I'm not interested in the literary competition any more, so let's stick to what we said and go to the café."

But the others were all eaten up with curiosity about whether Evi would win the competition with *my* story, so in the end we settled it that Luce and I would go down to the café, and the other four would stay at school to see what Ms Chambers announced.

Next, we had the problem of actually getting to the café. Luce's mum had sent a note to excuse Luce and to explain about the cookery competition, but obviously I couldn't risk sending a note as well, so I decided to risk skiving instead. I'd have to be careful because if anyone caught me, I'd be in big trouble from Mum and Dad *and* from school.

I didn't wait for the end-of-lunch bell to go. Instead, I kept my eye on the school windows as subtly as I could, while moving closer and closer to the exit and finally slipping out.

Luce walked out blatantly above five minutes later and we hurried down to the café, feeling very nervous and curious.

"What if she's there?" Luce asked me the moment we'd set off.

"She's sure to be there," I replied.

"Yeah, so what should I say to her?"

"Well, I don't know. Just say what you feel. Tell her how angry you are with her for taking Harry and making him suffer."

"There's only one problem."

"What?"

"I'm not angry any more."

"What!"

"I can't help it. My anger was monumentally enormous at first, but now it's just kind of gone," Luce told me almost apologetically.

I looked at her and couldn't believe what I was hearing. I mean, we'd waited nearly three weeks for the pleasure of cornering Evi and giving her a real rocket, and now here was Luce calmly telling me that she didn't actually feel like it any more.

"Well, perhaps you'll feel differently when you see her," I said, thinking as I said it how pathetic I sounded.

"Just think, she may be here right now, in this kitchen," said Luce, as she placed her hand slowly on the back door to the kitchen ready to push it open. We gave each other a long look, then I said, "Go on, you've got to do it sometime."

So she did.

My heart was beating much faster than usual as we both scanned the kitchen quickly the moment we were inside the door.

"Not arrived yet," said Kevin, realizing instantly who we were looking for.

The relief that Luce and I both felt must have been obvious even to Kevin. Then, a second, later, the door opened again and in came a boy who looked about the same age as us. He had red hair and freckles and gave us both a big grin and said hello straightaway.

"Hello, Jonathan," Kevin said, wiping his hand on his apron and extending it to Jonathan. "Nice to see you. Well done!"

Jonathan seized Kevin's hand and shook it rather vigorously, which seemed to amuse Kevin.

"Let me introduce you to Lucy Edmunson, who is one of the other two finalists," Kevin went on, and Jonathan came striding over to Luce and gave her the energetic hand–shaking treatment.

"And this is Luce's friend, Jaimini," said Kevin. "We're still waiting for the third finalist to turn up."

Kevin told Luce and Jonathan that they might as well start. "It's not a race," he explained with a grin. "As long as you're ready by three forty-five, that's fine. Then we'll have the judging by my friend and fellow chef, Martin Rhuanna, and this will be followed by the announcement. Martin will be here shortly."

So Luce and Jonathan started setting out all their ingredients and in no time at all they had both got totally absorbed in what they were doing. I whispered to Luce that I'd wait in the café for her, but she didn't want to face Evi on her own, so in the end I stayed and helped Kevin. Every time the door from the café opened it gave me a heart attack, but it was always Jan or Mark, and by twenty to three I began to consider the possibility that maybe Evi wasn't planning on showing up at all.

Noticing Kevin glancing at the clock, I asked him what would happen if Evi didn't actually appear.

"Then it would be between Luce and Jonathan," he replied with a shrug, and just then Jan came in yet again and went straight over to Luce, looking extremely serious and worried.

"I've just had a very odd phone call," said Jan softly. "It was someone to say that she'd taken Harry to the wheelie bin and that you'd know what that meant. Do you?"

Jan was looking very concerned and poor Luce immediately turned pale, making her freckles stand out.

"I'll go," I quickly offered. "I can deal with it, Luce."

"What's going on, Luce?" asked Jan.

"Did she say anything else?" Luce answered with her own question.

"Well…"

"What, Jan? Please tell me."

"I've just tried to get hold of your mum actually, but there was no reply."

"Why? What did that girl say?" Luce demanded, almost hysterically.

Jan's eyes darted to left and right, which was a habit of hers whenever she didn't know what to say. The desperate look in Luce's eyes must have made her decide.

"She said this time you'd ... better get there quickly..."

Luce and I both gasped and Luce's hand went straight to her mouth as though she was trying to stop an even bigger gasp escaping.

"She also said that she'd blocked off the breathing hole," Jan went on in scarcely more than a whisper.

"I've got to go," Luce said, dropping the whisk into the bowl of eggy flan mixture that was all ready to be poured into the pastry case that she'd made.

"Look, Luce, I'll go. You stay here or you'll lose your chance of winning."

"I can't, Jaimini. It's no good. I'd never forgive myself if anything happened to him and I hadn't even bothered to go and see for myself. Sorry, Kevin," she said, then she whipped off her apron, which sent a white powdery cloud over Jonathan, who had been listening with his mouth open. He must have suddenly realized that he was being rather rude, so he quickly got on with his cooking as though his life depended on it.

There was no stopping Luce when she was in this mood, so the best I could do was to go with her, and off we went, leaving Jan, Kevin and Jonathan staring speechlessly after us.

160

Luce and I aren't as fit as Andy and Fen, so we half walked, half jogged for ages without saying a single word. If Luce was anything like me, though, her brain was going at three hundred revs per minute, and suddenly I realized something blindingly obvious. I stopped and put a hand on Luce's arm to stop her, too.

"We're *so* stupid," I began. "I bet this is Evi's way of getting you out of the café so she can go in there and win the competition."

"But Jan wouldn't allow that!" Luce pointed out protestingly.

"But Jan doesn't know it's Evi, does she?" I pointed out.

"What do you mean?"

I didn't answer because I could see that the truth was slowly dawning on Luce.

"An anonymous phone call... Nothing at all to connect the voice to Evi Bligh ... and no reason why Jan should make any connection..." Luce stared straight ahead of her, looking daggers at the thin air.

"If only we'd told Jan or Kevin about what Evi did to Harry," I said, slowly and hopelessly.

"But the fact remains, if Harry's in that wheelie bin with no air, I've got to get him out."

She had already started jogging again so I joined her, but still my brain was ticking away. After a little while we came to a phone box.

161

"Hang on a sec," I said, breathing quite heavily.

Luce didn't ask any questions, just came with me into the phone box and waited while I dialled her home number and reversed the charges.

"Oh Melanie, I thought you were out," I began, feeling shocked but really pleased to hear her voice.

"I've just got in. I was taking Harry for a walk. What can I do for you, Jaimini? Are you phoning from school?"

She sounded worried.

"What did you say, Melanie?"

"I said, 'What can I do for you'?"

"No, about Harry."

At that point Luce grabbed the phone from me. "Evi's put Harry in the bin again, Mum. You've got to go and get him out. Go now, in the car, quick!"

There was a pause, while Melanie was obviously speaking. I watched Luce's expression turn from desperate to disbelieving to rapturous.

"She's got him at home," she whispered to me, covering the mouthpiece. I nodded happily because I'd gathered that.

"Got to go, Mum. Bye!"

With that, Luce replaced the receiver and we both set off at the speed of light back to the café.

Chapter 10

It turned out that there was no way either of us could keep up our ambitious pace.

"I'm dead," Luce announced, slowing to a walk.

"Me too," I agreed. We looked at our watches and that did it. Our walk became a standstill because it was already twenty-five to four.

"It's no good," Luce said flatly. "That's completely ruined my chances. Martin will be judging by the time we get back and my great flan isn't even finished."

"Come on," I said, feeling a sudden surge of venom towards Evi that she could do this to my best friend. "Let's get back, and I'll tell the whole story to Jan and Kevin. Your flan was practically finished, anyway."

"But it's our word against Evi's, isn't it? Why should they believe us?"

"I don't know, but there's nothing to lose by at least *trying* to convince them, is there?"

We went in through the back door to the kitchen feeling a mixture of emotions. My main emotion was anger. I wanted to throttle Evi Bligh. For the second time that day our eyes flew round the kitchen, but once again there was no sign of Evi. Maybe it wasn't her who had made the phone call, or maybe it *was*, but she decided not to turn up at the café herself. Perhaps she wasn't bothered about winning, only about ruining Luce's chances.

Jan rushed in and immediately flew over to Luce to ask whether Harry was all right.

"We didn't get that far," Luce answered. "We phoned Mum on a sudden impulse of Jaimini's and she'd just got back from taking Harry for a walk."

"It was all a trick to get Luce out of here so that she couldn't win the competition," I went on.

As I'd been talking I'd also been looking round. On the table were three dishes, all cooked, all looking wonderful and all with a bit missing. Kevin was standing there with another very good-looking, tall, dark, bearded chef, who must have been Martin Rhuanna, and Jonathan was standing behind the dish which I knew was his – a sort of vegetable moussaka. If my expression was anything like Luce's, I must have been looking very puzzled.

"That's my flan!" she said. "Who finished it for me?"

"Evi Bligh," replied Jonathan. "She's a really nice girl."

"And whose is that?" went on Luce, ignoring Jonathan's words and pointing to the third dish on the table, which looked like a vegetable crumble.

"That's Evi's," replied Jan. "Where is she anyway? She was here a moment ago."

Of course, that had the immediate effect of making everyone else in the room look round, too. Everyone except Kevin, that is. He didn't say a word, and neither did I, but later when I thought back to that moment I realized that Kevin knew she wouldn't be coming back.

"Have you done the tasting yet, Kevin?" asked Luce.

"Nope, we've got a mouse in here who's nibbled a bit out of each dish," replied Kevin, sarcastically but not unkindly.

"I only asked because I'm so surprised that you haven't dropped down dead from food poisoning if Evi Bligh has had anything to do with my flan."

"Don't be silly, Luce," said Jan. "Evi would never dream of doing a thing like that. Anyway, all she did was pour the mixture that you'd already made into your pastry case, then Kevin put it in the oven for you, *and* took it out when it was cooked. I thought it was a really nice gesture of hers, personally. In fact, we all found her a lovely girl."

I noticed that Kevin pursed his lips at that point, and realized instantly that he didn't agree.

"That lovely girl is the one who made the phone call," I told Jan, feeling my temper mounting. "And where is she now, this lovely girl…? I'll tell you where. She's beat a hasty retreat because she knows she'll get found out if she stays here."

Jan looked at Kevin as if she didn't quite know what to do. On the one hand, she thought Evi was a perfectly nice girl, but on the other hand, things were beginning to look rather fishy.

"I must admeet," said Martin, speaking for the first time, with a strong Italian accent, "I found her a leetle odd."

"Odd? She's totally screwed up," Luce corrected poor Martin. "She punishes people for not being her friend. She even goes as far as punishing *their* friends. And when she's not doing that, she's manipulating things so that something goes terribly wrong in your life, and then *she*, the great Evi Bligh, steps in and makes it all right again. It's her way of trying to make you like her, but she's gone too far this time."

"So what 'as she done?" asked Martin, who was really getting involved with all the drama.

Luce was about to launch into another heavy story about Evi but Jan got in first.

"Sorry to spoil the fun but hadn't we better get this show on the road? There are quite a few people in the café who are waiting to see who has won this competition, you know."

"Quite right," agreed Kevin. "Bring the dishes through into the café," he said, with an encouraging smile for Luce and Jonathan. So those two each carried through their own dish, and Jan took Evi's. An unexpected burst of applause met our entry. I felt like a bit of an imposter so I quickly moved to the edge of the room, just near the door.

It seemed strange seeing lots of people all sitting at tables round the edge of the café, and all looking towards the centre table on which the three dishes were placed. Luce and Jonathan stayed in the middle with Kevin and Martin, but Jan moved over to join me.

"Welcome, everybody," began Kevin, addressing all the smiling, waiting people. "I have great pleasure in introducing my friend and fellow chef, Martin Rhuanna, who is judging this cookery competition."

At this point there was a lot of clapping and in the middle of that, the door opened, and in walked Melanie and Mum!

"Mum!" I gasped. "What are you doing out of bed?"

She put a finger to her lips and mouthed, "It's OK." But she couldn't say any more because Kevin was talking again.

"Martin and I have had a lot of fun with all this. In fact, we've both enjoyed ourselves so much that we've decided to make it a weekly event!"

Everybody laughed at Kevin's wit.

"Martin tells me it wasn't easy picking out three finalists," he went on, "but in the end he came up with Lucy Edmunson, Jonathan Weekes and Evi Bligh…"

I could see everyone craning their necks to try and see where Evi was. I also saw Luce and Melanie have a brief conversation with their eyes. It went like this.

"*What are* you *doing here? I thought I told you not to come.*"

"*Sorry, love, I couldn't resist it, but I'm glad I'm here. It's exciting, isn't it?*"

"*I'm not excited, I'm just worried that I'm going to disappoint you. You wait and see if I don't.*"

Mum had managed to whisper to me during the laughter that the doctor had said it was fine for her to lead a fairly normal life till the end of her pregnancy, but just to take things gently. She and Melanie had come in the car, at least!

"Unfortunately Evi Bligh is unable to be with us at the moment, but she was here to make this entry of hers" (he indicated it with his hand),

168

"and very nice it tastes, too."

"Verrrry nice," Martin put in, which made everyone laugh because of his strong Italian accent.

"Evi's entry is a leek and potato crumble," Kevin went on. "Jonathan's is a vegetable moussaka, and Lucy's made cheese and celery flan. All three dishes tasted quite delicious and Martin's had a great deal of difficulty coming to a final decision."

"But eventually," continued Martin, "after much deliberation and a leetle more tasting just to be sure, I chose my winner."

"And that winner is..." said Kevin.

I held my breath, and looked from Kevin to Martin to Kevin to Martin because it was anybody's guess which one of them would announce the winner.

"Lucy Edmunson!" Martin and Kevin announced simultaneously, as they punched the air dramatically.

Immediately everyone broke into loud applause and Luce looked as though she'd just heard the news that school had been banned for everyone over the age of twelve. I rushed over to her and gave her a big hug. As it happened Melanie had the same idea, so we sort of collided and all three hugged each other, which made all the clapping people break into laughter as well.

Then Jan gave Luce a hug and I felt really

sorry for Jonathan, even though Kevin and Martin were chatting away to him and he looked perfectly happy.

"Bad luck, Jonathan," I said to him.

"That's OK. Lucy deserved to win. Actually, Kevin let me have a taste of hers, and I have to admit, it was excellent."

I really liked the way Jonathan was so pleasant about it all. Some people would have gone off into a big sulk.

"The runners up each receive book tokens for ten pounds," Kevin went on, "but a cheque for a hundred pounds goes to Lucy Edmunson, as well as a kiss from her favourite chef." He was leaning towards Lucy, all ready to give her a kiss, but quick as a flash she moved away and stood right in front of Martin, who looked delighted and gave her a kiss on each cheek. Of course, that made the audience erupt with laughter, cheering and more clapping. Kevin didn't mind. He was pretending to be really upset, so Luce came back and gave him a kiss, too.

Then the door opened and in walked Fen, Andy, Leah and Tash. They were all looking as though they'd won the Lottery or something, but instead of rushing up to Luce as I thought they would, they came flying over to me. Luce, seeing their rapt expression, came to hear what they were about to say.

"You won, Jaimini!" they told us in unison. "You won the literary competition!"

"What?" I said, probably sounding totally dim.

"You won it!" they repeated, with even more enthusiasm.

"But I couldn't have done," I said, wondering what on earth they were on about. "Or do you really mean that Evi won with my story?" I went on despondently.

"No, no, not that story," Fen answered, beginning to sound exasperated. "The other one – *Sound Bites*!"

"But I didn't…"

I looked round uncomprehendingly at their grinning faces, and realized that each and every one of them had turned to Luce, who was looking distinctly blushworthy.

"Sorry, Jaimes," she said, "but I couldn't resist it. You were being so stubborn about entering that story, and we all agreed that it was brilliant, and I decided to enter it on your behalf, but that meant that you weren't allowed to enter your other story, otherwise you would have been disqualified. I know I should have told you, but I also knew that if I *did* tell you, you'd go berserk… Sorry."

"So that's why…"

"Yes, that's why everything," Tash finished off. "That's why Fen didn't get you that magazine,

Our Times, and why Luce's mum bought the last copy the next day."

"But we didn't take your copy out of your bag, honestly," Luce added.

"That must have been Evi," said Fen.

"Look, I'm really sorry, Jaimes, but I wanted you to have a wonderful surprise," Luce went on, looking as though she was about to burst into tears.

I suddenly realized that I wasn't showing my real feelings, because it was only just dawning on my poor tired brain that I really had won the competition. It didn't matter with which story, after all, did it? I was about to break into a big beam of utter happiness when I thought back to how cross I'd been with Luce, how I'd not understood the looks that kept passing between her and the others, how I'd misinterpreted the whole thing, and how badly that had affected our friendship.

So, my big happy beam never did appear, and Luce must have taken my lack of reaction for me not being able to forgive her for interfering with my life.

"Sorry," she murmured for the third time. "Oh, what a disaster!" And with that she turned and walked over to her mum, but, fortunately, I gathered my senses just in time and caught up with her before she got to Melanie.

"It's OK, honestly. I was just feeling sad for a moment about all we've both had to go through... It was such a total misunderstanding..."

Still Luce didn't look convinced, so I thought I'd leave her in no doubt at all. I stood on a chair and stepped on to a table and clapped my hands for silence. This was *very* out of character for me, I can tell you.

"I have an announcement to make," I began, then the moment the words were out of my mouth, I found I couldn't go on because it would have sounded as though I was blowing my own trumpet. I sort of trailed off and felt completely and utterly and helplessly embarrassed.

Then before I knew it, Luce had leapt up by my side and we were both gripping each other round the waist because it wasn't the biggest table in the world, and we were wobbling dangerously.

"No, *I* have an announcement to make," she took over smoothly. "This is my best friend, Jaimini Riva, and she has just won a different competition – a national literary competition, and it's a big, *big* deal! And I'm very proud of her!"

I waited until the clapping had died down before I spoke.

"But I couldn't have done it without Luce," I said. "I mean, I really couldn't!"

Then together we counted to three and jumped down to the floor right beside the others, who were all bursting with happiness. It was a wonderful moment. A moment when nothing else mattered!

The next day at school we learnt from the teachers that Evi Bligh had left our school and Cableden altogether.

"Her father's job means that they have to be continually on the move," Mrs Merle said. "It's very difficult – more difficult than you can imagine – to make friends under these circumstances," she went on.

We all looked at each other. We got the message, but we weren't in any hurry to change our minds about Evi Bligh.

Then later, in the café, I overheard this conversation between Jan and Kevin. They didn't know I was listening. Jan spoke first.

"I still think it's weird, Kevin, what Evi did."

"Yeah, me too."

"I mean, why did she go to all that trouble to stop Luce winning and then go to all that trouble to make sure she did?"

"Dunno. Beats me."

"But tell me honestly, Kevin, if Evi hadn't told you and Martin that she wouldn't accept first prize even if it was offered to her, would Martin have given it to her? Was she really the winner in Martin's view?"

There was a long pause.

"Yes, she was. Martin was very definite about that," Kevin replied. "He said that Luce was certainly a close second, but Evi would have won."

I haven't told Luce about that conversation, and I never will, but I can't help going over and over it in my mind. It's just one more thing to add to the mystery of Evi Bligh.

Join

Would you and your friends like to know more about Fen, Tash, Leah, Andy, Jaimini and Luce?

We have produced a special bookmark for you to use in your Café Club books. To get yours free, together with a special newsletter about Fen and her friends, their creator, author Ann Bryant, and advance information about what's coming next in the series, write (enclosing a self-addressed label, please) to:

The Café Club
c/o the Publicity Department
Scholastic Children's Books
Commonwealth House
1-19 New Oxford Street
London WC1A 1NU

We look forward to hearing from you!

The **CAFÉ** Club

**Make room for these delicious helpings of
the Café Club and meet the members:
Fen, Leah, Luce, Jaimini, Tash and Andy.
Work has never been so much fun!**

1: GO FOR IT, FEN!
Fen and her friends are fed up with being poor.
Then Fen has a *brilliant* idea – she'll get them all
jobs in her aunt's café! *Nothing* can get in the
way of the Café Club...

2: LEAH DISCOVERS BOYS
What with the Café Club, homework and the
Music Festival, Leah certainly hasn't got time for
boyfriends... Until Oliver comes on the scene...

3: LUCE AND THE WEIRD KID
Nothing's working out for Luce. She's been
grounded, her hair's gone purple and now this
weird kid's got her into deep trouble at the café...

4: JAIMINI AND THE WEB OF LIES
Jaimini's parents want to ruin her life by sending
her to a posh school. But the Café Club are
plotting to save her...

5: ANDY THE PRISONER
Andy's a prisoner at creaky old Grandma Sorrell's!
She's got to break out — and she knows *just* the
friends to help her...

6: TASH'S SECRETS
Tash has a secret *no one* must find out about. If they
do, Tash might lose her friends for ever...

7: FEN'S REVENGE
Fen's having trouble with boys. She's out for
revenge, and the Café Club are right behind her...

8: LEAH IN TROUBLE
Leah needs cash, but Jan won't let her busk
in the Café. But then Jan falls ill, and
Hilda Salmon takes over...

9: LUCE'S BIG MISTAKE
Luce can't believe she's too big to play Annie in
the musical! She's determined to get the part,
whatever the cost...

Don't forget to come back for more!

HIPPO ANIMAL

*If you like animals, then you'll love
Hippo Animal Stories!*

Thunderfoot
Deborah van der Beek
When Mel finds the enormous, neglected horse
Thunderfoot, she doesn't know it will change her
life for ever...

Vanilla Fudge
Deborah van der Beek
When Lizzie and Hannah fall in love with the same
dog, neither of them will give up without a fight...

A Foxcub Named Freedom
Brenda Jobling
An injured vixen nudges her young son away from her.
She can sense danger and cares nothing for herself –
only for her son's freedom...

Pirate the Seal
Brenda Jobling
Ryan's always been lonely – but then he meets Pirate and at last he has a real friend...

Animal Rescue
Bette Paul
Can Tessa help save the badgers of Delves Wood from destruction?

Take Six Puppies
Bette Paul
Anna knows she shouldn't get attached to the six new puppies at the Millington Farm Dog Sanctuary, but surely it can't hurt to get just a *little* bit fond of them...

HIPPO ANIMAL

Midnight Dancer
Elizabeth Lindsay

Ride into adventure with Mory and her pony,
Midnight Dancer

Book 1: Midnight Dancer
Mory is thrilled when she finds the perfect pony. But will
she be allowed to keep her?

Book 2: Midnight Dancer: To Catch a Thief
There's a thief with his eye on Mory's mother's sapphire
necklace – and it's down to Mory and Midnight Dancer
to save the day…

Book 3: Midnight Dancer: Running Free
Mory and Dancer have a competition to win. But they
also have a mystery to solve…

Book 4: Midnight Dancer: Fireraisers
There's trouble on Uncle Glyn's farm – because there's a
camper who loves playing with fire. Can Mory and
Dancer avert disaster?

Look out for:

Book 5: Midnight Dancer: Joyriders
Book 6: Midnight Dancer: Winners and Losers

R.L.Stine

Reader beware, you're in for a scare!
These terrifying tales will send shivers up your spine:

Reader beware – here's THREE TIMES
the scare!

Look out for these bumper GOOSEBUMPS
editions. With three spine-tingling stories by
R.L. Stine in each book, get ready for three
times the thrill ... three times the scare ...
three times the GOOSEBUMPS!

GOOSEBUMPS COLLECTION 1
Welcome to Dead House
Say Cheese and Die
Stay Out of the Basement

GOOSEBUMPS COLLECTION 2
The Curse of the Mummy's Tomb
Let's Get Invisible!
Night of the Living Dummy

GOOSEBUMPS COLLECTION 3
The Girl Who Cried Monster
Welcome to Camp Nightmare
The Ghost Next Door

GOOSEBUMPS COLLECTION 4
The Haunted Mask
Piano Lessons Can Be Murder
Be Careful What You Wish For